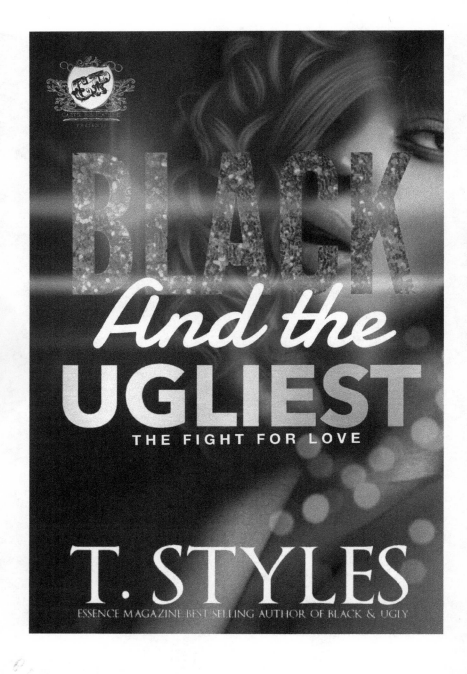

BLACK And the UGLIEST

THE FIGHT FOR LOVE

T. STYLES

ESSENCE MAGAZINE BEST SELLING AUTHOR OF BLACK & UGLY

ARE YOU ON OUR EMAIL LIST?

SIGN UP ON OUR WEBSITE

www.thecartelpublications.com

OR TEXT THE WORD:

CARTELBOOKS TO 22828

FOR PRIZES, CONTESTS, ETC.

BLACK AND THE UGLIEST

T. STYLES

WWW.THECARTELPUBLICATIONS.COM

BLACK AND THE UGLIEST

BLACK AND THE UGLIEST:
THE FIGHT FOR LOVE

By

T. STYLES

Library of Congress Control Number: 2018947299

ISBN 10: 1945240970

ISBN 13: 978-1945240973

Cover Design: Bookslutgirl.com

www.thecartelpublications.com
First Edition
Printed in the United States of America

What's Up Fam,

I only have one important message I want to get off my chest to you with this letter. It's about depression. Fam, I know what it means to be depressed and feel like you don't know where to turn. In life, we face obstacles, some more than others, but please know that you are never alone and someone is always going through something too. If you feel like all hope is lost and you have nowhere left to turn, reach out and talk to someone. Here's the number for the National Suicide Prevention Hotline: 1-800-273-8255. Help sometimes can be in the last place you think to look. God Bless!

Now that I got that out, let me get into the book in hand, "Black and The Ugliest: The Fight For Love". I can't say enough about this book. I was soooo fucking happy to have my Miss Wayne and Parade back! Their story always puts a huge smile on my face because along with Kelsi (A Hustler's Son), I've known them the longest from T. Styles' literary works and I really do love them. The mess they get into this time is non-stop, so sit back and enjoy yourself! I know I did.

With that being said, keeping in line with tradition, we want to give respect to a vet or trailblazer paving the way. In this novel, we would like to recognize:

THE WASHINGTON CAPITALS

The Washington Capitals are a NHL Hockey Team that just won their first Stanley Cup Championship in the history of the franchise. Now, I'm not a hockey fan but I was born in D.C. and can appreciate the major accomplishment that this is. I watched a few of the games during this series and was actually very entertained! They played their hearts and souls out! Congratulations Caps! Ya'll truly deserve this honor!

Aight, get to it. I'll catch you in the next book.

Be Easy!

Charisse "C. Wash" Washington
Vice President
The Cartel Publications

BLACK AND THE UGLIEST

www.thecartelpublications.com

www.facebook.com/publishercwash

Instagram: publishercwash

www.twitter.com/cartelbooks

www.facebook.com/cartelpublications

Follow us on Instagram: Cartelpublications

#CartelPublications

#UrbanFiction

#PrayForCeCe

#PrayForT

#WashingtonCapitals

CARTEL URBAN CINEMA'S WEB SERIES

BMORE CHICKS
@ Pink Crystal Inn

NOW AVAILABLE:

Via

YOUTUBE
And
DVD
(Season 2 Coming Soon)

www.youtube.com/user/tstyles74

www.cartelurbancinema.com

www.thecartelpublications.com

BLACK AND THE UGLIEST

#BlackandtheUgliest

PROLOGUE

WASHINGTON, DC

The moon was in rare form as it hovered above the filthy, grungy water that made up the Potomac River, causing it to shine in a liquid blue hue. A little to the right, on a patchy land that Chocolate City called Hains Point, two people stood on their knees, their gaze toward the river.

Their fate unclear.

Standing above them, a gunman aimed the warm barrel of a .45 in their direction, which had already been fired once as a warning shot indicating that he alone was in charge.

After what seemed like an eternity, slowly a black Impala rolled up in the parking lot some ways over from the group, the brightness of the headlights made the gunman squint slightly to see who was arriving. Normally policemen circled the tourist trap but a bomb threat had been called in not even three miles ahead to a government building, which required all available officers on deck. Which the Gunman was well aware of because he made the call.

BLACK AND THE UGLIEST

When the car parked, the lights went out, placing the scene as it was before its arrival.

Dark.

Scary.

Uncertain.

Slowly the Passenger and Driver eased out, carefully toward the trio.

Observant, the Driver glared at the Gunman, believing that if he tried hard enough he could knock him to the ground and end this madness once and for all.

"Don't be stupid!" The Gunman suggested, aiming at The Visitors and then back at the people on their knees. "I'm feeling kinda nervous right now. Don't make me kill everybody out this bitch before you have a chance to hear me out."

The Driver's hands went up into the air. "I'm unarmed." He paused. "Please don't do anything crazy."

The Gunman aimed at The Passenger. "Me too."

The Passenger's throat cleared. "Me...me too."

The Gunman returned his weapon onto the men on their knees and laughed. "Let me ask yah something right quick."

"I'm listening," The Driver said.

"You wouldn't happen to have a little liquor in the ride would you?" He snickered awkwardly. "Seeing as how at least one of you niggas gonna die today." He laughed hysterically. "We might as well drink to pouring blood."

CHAPTER ONE

LOS ANGELES, CALIFORNIA

PARADE

"I don't care what ya'll say," I yelled to my stylists in my salon *Silky Kinks*. I was sweeping hair off the floor and talking shit to them at the same time, which was a regular practice for us. "If this body starts falling apart Jay would have a fucking fit, I'm serious. Every night he talks about how he loves after all these years I still keep my shit tight." I swept the hair into a dustpan. "So a bitch needs maintenance. Trust me."

"I just can't believe he don't know you doing it," Bianca said as she twisted her client's hair. She specialized in all things faux locs and her clientele was serious and kept her bills paid and her lifestyle nice. Even though she came from India she taught herself about black hair texture and in no time was on top here in L.A. "Lipo puts you down for a few days. Especially with the drainage. Jay should know something is — "

"Nah, whenever I get lipo I stay at Wayne's." I tossed the loose strands of hair in the trash. "Because you right." I paused. "The way that man likes to touch

on me he would feel that little plastic ball and be like —
"

"Parade!" Someone yelled.

When I turned around I was looking at Lucky. And since I fired this bitch a few days ago I was definitely shocked. She was wearing a plain white t-shirt, tight blue jeans and red brown thong sandals. Her outfit was majorly off because Lucky never came out the house in less than the best.

"What you doing here?" Sirena asked her, walking in front of me in a protective motion. "Parade got rid of you." She folded her arms over her chest and awaited an answer.

Me too.

Sirena had been with me for the entire four years since my business took off. And since she looked so much like Sky, my childhood friend who made me feel bad for my chocolate complexion, at first I didn't like her. They even shared the same light skin. It was so bad that I almost didn't hire her until I realized they couldn't be more different.

"Stay out of it, Sirena!" Lucky screamed. "I'm not talking to you!" Lucky walked further into the shop. "And I'm here because the way this black bitch fired me was wrong! I didn't even get a chance to let my clientele know I didn't work here anymore."

"Lucky," Bianca said in a soft voice. "You were stealing money from all of us. Nobody would trust you enough to let you square up with your clients."

Silence.

When my gaze lowered I realized she was holding a switchblade. With one button press the blade was pointed in my direction. "Lucky, please don't do this," I said. The situation got out of hand quick. "I have a family who—"

"What about my fucking family?" She yelled. "What about my life? You didn't care about that did you?" She paused. "Karma is about to hit you so hard. I had a dream and everything you love is gonna be taken." She laughed hysterically.

Suddenly Lucky's hair was yanked from behind. When I blinked I saw it was courtesy of Miss Wayne who was standing behind her. I thought that was him in my peripheral vision when he first walked in my shop but too much was happening. I didn't know he could move so quickly but in the seconds it took for him to enter the doorway, it took fewer seconds to bring Lucky down.

"This bitch got me out here...sweating and...looking a fool." Wayne placed his knee in her throat, snatched the knife from her and tossed it across the shop. It spun on the floor next to the door. My stylists and me rushed to help keep her down. "What's wrong with you, Lucky? Huh?" He asked looking down at her. "Do you realize how hard it was for me to squat down on this floor with these tight ass pants?"

He looked up at us and we broke out into laughter.

"Fuck so funny?" He asked. "And stop standing around looking pretty! Call the police!"

PARADE

We were sitting in Miss Wayne's navy blue BMW drinking coffee from Starbucks. I don't know what was with the people in this town but they couldn't seem to live without it.

"Thanks for helping me back there," I said to him. "She acting like I did something wrong when she was the one stealing from me."

He waved his hand. "Fuck that. You my friend and you know I'm gonna always be there for you. Always."

He rifled through his brown Louis Vuitton purse, removed a comb and tamed his hair. The style he was rocking now was perfect for his face. The sides and back of his head were shaved but he wore the top in a long bang, which he swooped to the side over his left eye.

"But why are you here?" I paused. "Don't get me wrong, I'm glad you came when you did but normally you call first. We doing lunch or something?"

"Oh yes, that's what I wanted. Danny ran into Jay the other day." He looked at me, shook his head and fixed his hair again.

I moved uneasily in my seat. "Well...what happened?"

"Don't worry, doll," he continued pointing at me with the comb. "Luckily for you I already told Danny to tell tale of you staying over our house for a few days last week, so we kept your lie alive." He paused. "But, baby, you gotta stop fucking with your body with all these surgeries, Parade. The man gonna find out!"

I leaned back toward the window and glared at him. "This from the great Miss Wayne?" I said. "As many tucks as you do." I pointed at him. "Fuck outta here with all your madness."

"Bitch, I'm a queen!" He yelled. "Maintenance is not only necessary it's a requirement. Being a man with a waist this small don't come easy. You gotta pay for her!"

I looked him over. "And you are snatched."

"Thank you!" He curtsied in his seat. "Thank you!" He paused and took a big breath. "But seriously, you know how Jay feels about surgery. He loves you just the way you are."

"Miss Wayne, please stop." I sighed.

"Stop what?" He paused, dropping his comb back into his purse. "Giving it to you straight?" He folded his arms over his chest. "Don't forget, I'm the only one in this town who knew you from the Quincy Manor days." He paused. "That means I'm in touch with the real Parade and I don't want this place bringing light to old habits." He leaned closer. "Habits picked up from folks more insecure than you."

"You sound crazy."

He stared harder.

I knew where he was going. "Wayne, the drugs were a one time thing. After the last lipo the pain was worse than before and I used a little something to stop the feeling that's all. So please don't act like I'm an addict."

"Honey…you used a little heroin."

"I know I did! And I was strong enough to get off of it."

"Next time you might not be able to."

"Won't be a next time."

"All I'm saying is that I don't want you trying to change yourself into a different version of one of the walking dolls we see out here. Don't forget, I had to stop you from lightning your skin."

"It was a chemical peel! Not a brightener."

"I don't know what it was, Parade…to tell you the truth. All I know is you been comparing yourself to people out here and I need that to stop." He paused. "Not only because you the baddest bitch this town has ever seen, but also because if you not careful you may lose your husband, your family and your life."

I frowned. That was the second time today someone said I might lose it all. "You reaching ain't you? Why would surgery make me lose everything?" I laughed once.

"Am I?" He put his hands on his hips. "Plus I'm not just talking about the surgeries. Fuck the surgeries. I'm talking about the way you think. Lately it ain't been rational and I'm afraid you're gonna make the wrong choices. Choices that'll fuck up everything around you."

I looked down. "I'm not saying I agree with you but I have a feeling I may be losing Jay already."

"Nonsense."

"I'm serious. That's why I've been running back to the surgeon to get this tucked and that tucked. I would work out more but I'm at the shop so many hours that there's no time." I took a deep breath. "It's our anniversary and he's not even answering his phone, Wayne. Wasn't in the bed when I rolled over this morning either. He's sneaking around and..." I tried to push the tears away. "If it wasn't for my kids making me breakfast and lifting my spirits I might have stayed home from work." I looked into his eyes. "Do you think he found another woman? Prettier than me? Better than me? Because not a bitch alive would do the things I would do for him, Wayne. Not one."

He grabbed me into a one-arm hug. "Let's not expect the worst just yet. All across town we be hearing how bitches be trying to take a stab at your man and each got the same story to report back to Hoe Central. And that is that he shoots each and every one of them the fuck DOOOWWWNN." He paused. "Now

I don't know what's going on with him lately but let's wait until it reveals itself and you just stay prayed up."

"I pray all the time. Don't seem like prayers are getting answered though." I sighed deeply and looked out the window. When I saw Bianca walking toward the car from the shop I took another deep breath. I was emotionally exhausted. "Aw, shit, fake like you in a heated conversation with me."

"Say no more." He cleared his throat and pointed at me with both index fingers. "BITCH, AND ANOTHER THING..."

KNOCK. KNOCK.

Bianca knocked on the window and I took a deep breath and rolled it down. "Now's not a good time, Bianca. Me and Wayne talking about something serious."

She looked in the car and nodded. "Oh, yeah, um, I understand." She paused. "I was just hoping when you're done we'd be able to talk today like you said." She smiled. "Remember? You postponed it until today?"

"Like I said, now is not a good time."

She nodded. "I understand."

When she walked away I rolled the window up and we busted out laughing. "I don't know what that's all about but that woman is stunning for the kids."

I nodded. "She wants me to go in on some business with her on—"

"Parade," Miss Wayne said, his eyes wide as he looked in front of him.

"What's wrong?" I placed my hand on my heart.

"Where's your fucking car?"

I looked at my reserved parking space and my jaw dropped. "Somebody stole my shit!"

CHAPTER TWO
MISS WAYNE

Pulling a single key out of my pocket, I let myself into Parade's 10,000 square foot home in Ladera Heights, California, an upscale African-American neighborhood for the blacks with a coin.

I was holding a pan of five blend macaroni and cheese that my friends Dayshawn, Adrian and Chris forgot to remind me to bring when we were at home earlier tonight. That's why if you wanted something done you really had to do it for yourself.

I made the dish, one of many, for Parade and Jay's anniversary party that was going down now. And although my house was no slouch, half this size actually, I never got over how luxurious their home was when I pulled up and definitely when I walked inside.

The moment I pushed through the double doors I saw it was flooded with people holding champagne flutes in hand. Everyone seemed happy but I didn't spot the couple of the hour anywhere.

Where were they?

After all we were there for them and it took me forever to get ready. I wanted all to go down as planned. My friends and me ran a very popular restaurant here in L.A. called *Turned Out Cuisine*, and so Parade hired us for the festivities. Trust me, baby, we didn't let her down. The food was the best.

I smiled when I saw the gold and silver balloons and how they meshed perfectly with the white and grey color theme throughout their home decor. I decorated most of the rooms in the house but what I loved was that even though they have children, they didn't darken out the place to cover for the messiness issues most kids bring. Instead the children hung out in their rooms or their area in the basement and behaved themselves accordingly while in the common areas. I know I made sure my daughter Shantay acted like she had some sense in our living room.

Which was a chore in and of itself.

When I walked into the kitchen I frowned when I saw Adrian and Chris kissing which must've meant Jay wasn't home. Trust me when I say this. Jay loves me but he doesn't love "us". That means he would never stand for the gays kissing in his home. Not only were my friends out of line, Adrian had even resorted to tying up his white button down shirt and was also

BLACK AND THE UGLIEST

wearing the bob wig that I specifically forbade him to showcase.

Dayshawn, who we called *Abercrombie Bitch* because he had a nice thin build and could make a pair of black pants and white shirt look like a fashion statement, saw me and shook his head.

"I already told them," Dayshawn said waving the air as he poured champagne into flutes that sat on a silver-serving tray. "But they didn't wanna listen."

"Girl, shut up," Adrian said waving his fingertips at him. "You need to—"

I snatched off his wig, literally, which silenced him instantly. "You can't be carrying on like this in this man's house." I tossed it to the floor and placed my hands on my hips. "What you trying to do? Get us all kicked out and not paid?"

"I thought we weren't supposed to hide who we are anymore," Chris said softly. Chris and Adrian had a very volatile relationship in the earlier days. The man beat her so much that she forgot she didn't love him. Afterwards they just stayed together out of convenience I guess.

"We not but—"

"He's still not here," Parade said rushing into the kitchen interrupting our dialog about her husband.

Her makeup was on point. Still, as she held champagne I wondered if this was the beginning of the breakdown of her life, especially since she'd given up alcohol years ago.

I pointed at it.

"It's non-alcoholic," Dayshawn interrupted. I turned around and looked at him. "I wouldn't play with your straight wife like that, Wayne."

I winked at him and ushered Parade out the kitchen. "Why you thinking the worst of me?" She asked as I removed the glass from her hand and placed it on a table in the hallway. "I'm done living on the wild side."

"Not thinking the worst," I said. "Just being me which means worrying about you."

"Wayne, we talking about my husband here." Her eyes were wide and I could tell she'd been crying. "Every time my phone rings I'm hoping it's him and..." She ran her hands down her face. "Why would he do me like this on our anniversary?" She paused. "Huh? I didn't even tell him that my car was probably stolen."

I took a deep breath.

"We have a beautiful home." She looked around. "A successful life and —"

"Love." I interrupted. "No matter what, you have love."

"I know we got love, Wayne." She began walking when the music got louder in the party so I followed her to her bedroom where it was quieter. "Sometimes you treat me like a child and—"

"I'm just making sure you remember love is more important because all of this is beautiful and I'm happy for you. Especially after knowing where we come from, but love is where it's at and—"

"I keep telling you that I feel like something bad is about to happen." Her eyes widened with fright, almost like she saw a ghost. "I feel like all of this has been a dream and now it's over."

She looked so certain that she started scaring me. I was about to say something to make her feel better when…

"I think Jay's here," Adrian said running into her bedroom while wearing the wig again. I glared at him and he snatched it off and then rolled his eyes. "A girl's got to look pretty doesn't she?"

"How many times do I have to tell you that it's not about you?" I shook my head and followed Parade out the door, stealing one last look at Adrian on the way out.

When we made it to the living room Jay was standing in the doorway. At 6'3 he was as fine as he was when we were kids back in Maryland. His black and Spanish heritage offered him thick black wavy hair and now he had grown a smooth black goatee, which he kept shaped up and on point always. With all that said he was obviously drunk. A large white Styrofoam cup sat in his hand and his body swayed as everybody, holding up champagne flutes, gathered around him.

Separating from the crowd Parade walked up to him...slowly. In all of the drama I didn't see the beautiful red dress clearly until that moment. When I say Parade got a body...Baby, I don't think you would understand unless you were in her presence. Standing only 5'5 her waist was tiny and she possessed an ass so fat it held spectator's attention long after she was gone.

Besides all of that, she was simply beautiful. Her dark chocolate skin against any type of lighting always glowed. Her small nose, her plush lips and her beautiful white smile made her noticeable the moment she walked into the room. But still, after all these years I think living in L.A. caused her to hate herself even more.

"Jay," Parade said looking him up and down. "What's going on?"

BLACK AND THE UGLIEST

"Hey...hey, baby." He took a gulp from his cup as he swayed a little. "You fine as fuck you know that?"

"Jay!" She said firmer. "Answer me!"

He looked down, took a deep breath and looked back up at her. "I fucked up, Parade. I fucked up so bad and I tried to fix it but it didn't..." He took a deep breath again. "Please forgive me but we lost everything. The house. The life. All of it."

I walked closer, careful to still give them space.

"What does that mean, Jay?" Parade asked. "I...we pay our mortgage so...I'm not—"

"They putting us out our home," he paused. "In two days."

CHAPTER THREE
JAY

She was asleep, naked, as I stared down at her in our bed. I always loved the way her chocolate skin looked against the white sheets, 'specially when she wasn't wearing clothes. She was everything to me and I fucked up. Maybe even lost her for good.

Even though she was mad my dick was hard so I crawled up behind her hoping to, well...you know.

Her breath was steady so I figured if I could make it inside, just for a second, she would forget 'bout our problems. Slowly I placed my hand on her butt cheek, pushed and then lifted it exposing her pink center. My tip was almost at it's destination and then...

"What you doing?" She asked angrily.

We played this game before and normally she knew what I wanted and let me live but this time she was serious. I wouldn't be getting no pussy tonight. She sat up against the headboard, yanked the covers and pulled them closer to her body, covering her breasts.

"You looked so sexy that—"

"I don't want you touching me, Jay." She looked down. "Not right now anyway." I sat in front of her and placed my hand on her covered knee. She knocked it off.

"Babes, what can I do? Huh?" I asked. "Whatever it is, it's done. Just please don't, don't look at me how you looking at me now."

"And how is that?"

"Disappointed."

She breathed deeply. "Well, keep your eyes off me then because I have nothing else for you." She crawled out of bed, her meaty ass cheeks moving up and down.

I repositioned my dick because if she saw me hard she would flip, believing that I found her anger trivial. She stomped toward her purple robe hanging on our door and I ran behind her, gripped her around her waist and placed my cheek on the top of her head. "Please don't leave me, Parade." I walked in front of her. "I know I fucked up but I'm begging you not to leave. Not to leave us. We can work this out. Trust me."

"And why shouldn't I? We have three kids, Jay. Three! What were you thinking putting all of the money and everything we own in financial investments?" She paused. "I told you one time too many that a sure thing was never really sure!"

She walked away and flopped down at the foot of the bed. Her robe hung open revealing her chocolate breasts and all I wanted was to suck them, lay her down and make love.

"Listen, Landon, Logan and Ella gonna be good." I assured her. "I'm their father and —"

She laughed.

I walked up to her. "What's funny?"

"The twins are thirteen and Ella is nine." She paused. "All three of them have heavy social lives, Jay. And Logan has a girlfriend. How can you say everything will be alright when they'll be forced to leave everything they love? How can —"

"Ma, you cool?" Landon asked entering the doorway. He tucked his hands inside the front pockets of his red Polo pajama pants. Parade pulled her robe closed. "Logan said we have to leave. Is it true?"

"Son, I'm talking to your mother right now." I said. "I'll explain everything later."

"But —"

"Landon, go back to your room!" I roared. "Now."

He looked at her once and walked off.

I took a deep breath and focused back on Parade.

Despite this time, whenever I saw my boys I smiled with pride. With silky black hair and brown skin they were the best parts of my wife and me combined. Still, there were some things about Landon I was concerned with. One of the issues was his over protectiveness of his mother. The other issue was too much too talk about and I hoped I'd never have to face it.

"You love pushing him away," she said to me. "I really wish you weren't so hard on him."

I rolled my eyes. "That's my blood, Parade. The last thing I want is to push him away." I paused. "He just has to understand that you my wife and he's my son. Sometimes because you baby him so much I think he forgets. Regardless, when I tell him to do something it must be done."

"I'm not letting you do this." She jumped up and tied her robe together while moving for the door.

"Do what?"

"Change things around on me. At the end of the day you invested all of our money in Bitcoin and when shit failed you put a mortgage on our home and a bill on my car without telling me. Now we don't have anything and have to leave! You failed me as a husband and I will never forgive you." She stormed out and slammed the door behind herself.

I was gut punched.

Devastated.

More than anything, she was right.

I flopped on the edge of the bed and placed my face in my palms before running them downward and clutching them in front of me. I don't care what happened I had to get us put back on. They were my responsibility and at the end of the day I failed them as a man. She was accurate as fuck which is why it hurt more.

I was just about to make some phone calls when the door opened and Ella walked inside. Her hair was black, wild and curly and her skin tone was closer to mine than Parade's. She was beautiful and loved me more than anything. It's like she saw the best in me no matter what.

"Papi, are you okay?" She sat on the edge of the bed and hugged me.

"Everything will be fine, Ella."

"But I had a dream."

I frowned. "What about?"

"That you were going to die." She gripped me again and started crying. "Please, papi don't go. Don't leave us."

CHAPTER FOUR
PARADE

My head was throbbing. As I twisted my client's locs, every time I looked up I saw my hairdressers staring at me. Although *Silky Kinks* had six hairdressers I was closest to Bianca and Sirena, and still I wanted them both to leave me alone. To give me just one ounce of privacy. But when my client left and the shop was empty I could tell by the look in their eyes it wouldn't happen.

"Parade, you know I have the building we just bought," Sirena said walking up to me. "You and Jay are more than welcome to stay in one of the apartments until you get on your feet. I really don't mind. It would be my — "

I laughed loudly and shook my head, before grabbing the broom on the side of the wall and sweeping.

"What's funny?" Sirena asked.

"You know me and my kids not moving into no apartment," I assured her. "Besides, Jay gonna work it out. We talked about it already."

"I have no doubt." Sirena sighed. "I just wanted you to know that—"

"I'm not a fucking charity case!" I yelled looking at them both. "I don't need saving. All I need is for the both of you to do your jobs and stay out of my business. Can you do that or not?"

"Parade," Bianca said with wide eyes. "Look." She was pointing outward.

When I faced the door I saw a man in a black suit holding a white folded up piece of paper. Two police officers stood behind him. They all moved inside with the type of walk that made me feel small in my own establishment. "Which one of you is..." Black Suit unfolded the paper. "Parade Hernandez?"

I cleared my throat. "I...I mean...I am."

He walked over to me and handed me the sheet. "We are seizing this shop and all of its possessions for the bank."

I placed my hand over my heart. "W...why?"

"That would've gotten explained over a year ago if you showed up to court." He paused. "Perhaps you should ask your husband though. However, at this point you have 90 days to come up with all of the money owed or...well...you know the rest." He looked over my head at my stylists. "I need everyone out immediately. Only take your personal belongings. This business is now the property of Hill Creek National Bank."

PARADE

When I woke up I was in the passenger's seat of Wayne's car. I wiped my mouth with the back of my hand and sat up. My lips were dry and my tongue parched from yelling and crying. "Where we going?" I looked out the window.

"How you feeling?" He asked as he continued to drive.

I sighed and remembered what happened at my shop. Jay even put my business up as collateral. This was crazy. "How do you have everything one moment and nothing the next?"

He took a deep breath.

"He lied to me, Wayne," I said as tears flowed down my face. "More than anything he—"

"Is your husband."

"And I understand all that!" I yelled. "But he embarrassed me in front of my friends and—"

"What is happening to you?" He asked as he frowned at me.

I looked away.

"What has L.A. done to all of the work we did in Maryland?" He continued. "Because lately all you seem to be concerned with is this lifestyle and how you look." He paused. "For all we know your love for living in luxury may be the reason Jay made some bad decisions."

"Wait, so this my fault now?"

"Never said that. I just want you to be aware."

I laughed. "It's funny how you taking up for him but when I gave him your offer, for us and the kids to live at your house, he said no. Didn't want Landon and Logan around a bunch of faggies." I paused. "His words not mine. But you keep taking up for your mans if you want to."

He smiled and shook his head.

I felt immediate guilt.

"I'm sorry."

"You don't have to say what's evident," he said. "You sorry as shit."

"Wayne!"

"What?" He pulled over and parked in front of somebody else's house even though mine was on the next block. "What were you about to say?" He continued. "That I'm wrong for agreeing with you?"

I ran my hand down my face. "I don't know what I'm going to do," I cried. "I don't...I don't know..."

"You hold your family closer, Parade. That's what you do. You don't bring more space in between you all by placing blame on your husband. It won't help right now."

I shook my head and took a deep breath. "God has taken everything from me."

"How can you be sure? Maybe he gave everything to you by taking away things you don't need right now." He paused. "You went from having nothing to having everything and it looks like you still have no idea who you are. And that makes you ill prepared to be handling money. Cash just shows the worst in us if we aren't strong." I looked at him.

"We'll see." I said.

"At least now I know where your car went."

My eyes widened. "You do?"

He nodded. "I was on my way to the shop to tell you I made some connections on the streets about your ride. After a few calls to my family at the House Of

Dreams it became apparent that your car was repossessed. If you would've called the police we would've found out."

"I know. Was too afraid to face it. "I took a deep breath and looked out my window. "My car is in Jay's name but his truck is in his mother's. That's why he still has his wheels."

"Yep."

Suddenly Wayne grew quiet and I looked over at him. He was squinting and looking ahead. "What's wrong?" I asked.

"Is all them people going into your house?"

My heart banged inside the walls of my chest.

They were.

CHAPTER FIVE
JAY

There had to be at least twenty niggas in my house. Taking pictures off the walls, sculptures off tables and electronics off brackets. The only thing they didn't take was the clothing and I had put most of our stuff in the U-Haul trailer while I waited on my wife.

To be honest I was ready to leave.

"Pops, where we gonna live?" Landon asked walking up to me. Logan was next to him on his iPhone texting. He was probably hitting up his girl who was a bitch. I hated the fuck out that little ass broad.

"Back to Maryland for now."

Logan looked up at me, his eyes wide. "Maryland? But what about my girl?" He asked. "And my friends?"

"What about 'em?" I glared.

"Man, I hate you!" He yelled, running out the house. "I FUCKING HATE YOU!"

Landon looked up at me and sighed. "I'ma go look for him."

I was trying to keep my calm but all this shit was weighing on me. Like I knew I needed to do something but didn't know what. Sometimes the twins blew me. When I felt someone holding my hand I looked down and saw Ella. "I don't care where we go," she said. "As long as we're together." It was like she could hear my thoughts.

I smiled at her and ruffled her hair. Digging in my pocket I handed her the keys to my Suburban. "Go wait in the truck. We staying at a hotel tonight before we take the trip."

She took them from me and walked away smiling.

Just then Parade and Wayne walked through the door. I met them halfway as movers were entering and leaving the house with authority. "What's happening now?" Parade asked, tears running down her face.

"We talked about this." I paused. "You already know."

"Is there anything I can do?" Wayne asked.

I shook my head no, too ashamed to face him. Plus, don't get me wrong. I fucked with Wayne, I really did. But there was a lot I had to stop when we first got here. Like Parade calling him Miss Wayne when he was around my kids and letting them go over his house. Gay men ran in and out that bitch and one time I caught Landon playing with one of his wigs in our house, which I had no idea how he managed to take from Wayne's crib as tight as he was with them things.

Anyway, what Wayne does in his own life is his business but I couldn't have it around my family. That's why we couldn't live with him even if it was temporary.

"Okay, well let me know." He took a deep breath and hugged Parade. "This is happening for a reason, Parade. I feel it."

She snatched away from him and ran upstairs.

When she was gone he looked at me. "I don't know how you got this low but you gotta fix this shit, Jay. It's the worst I've ever seen her and I don't like it."

"I know what I have to do, Wayne."

He placed the handle of his purse in the middle of his forearm while both hands sat on his hips. "And I'm not saying you don't. What I do know is that if you don't have a plan that works, you're about to lose everything." He glared at me. "Now think on that with your arrogant ass." He turned around and stomped out the door, knocking into a mover in the progress.

I waved the air and went to find my wife.

THE NEXT MORNING
JAY

It was a rough night at Motel Chaz and although I wasn't looking forward to us staying with my mother, I was relieved to be getting away from L.A. Everywhere I went people knew me and heard about us losing our home and businesses. I just wanted a break but it wouldn't be easy.

For starters my mother and wife didn't get along. Mainly because she never got over the fact that my wife was dark skinned. She wanted me with a white or light woman but I couldn't help who I fell in love with. She said the darker the skin the harder the journey but I didn't see it that way unless people believed they were inferior because of it.

Besides, my wife is beautiful and the children we had together is a testament of what happens when Latin and black culture meet. Still, we had no choice.

My kids were already in the truck waiting on the long ride ahead. I couldn't afford plane tickets for all of us so we had to drive. I slid into the driver's seat when

BLACK AND THE UGLIEST

suddenly I saw Wayne's navy blue BMW pull up. Danny, his husband or whatever he called him these days, was driving and Wayne was in the passenger's seat.

They parked next to the car said a few things to each other and looked at me. I was confused. I waved at Danny and Wayne slid out with a duffle, said a few words to Danny and he pulled off quickly. I take it Danny was hot about something.

Parade came out our room's door and walked up to Wayne. I could see and hear them from the window.

"What you doing here?" Parade asked him.

"You got three kids and a situation," Wayne said. "You need my help and I'm gonna be there for you."

"What about Shantay?" Parade asked. "You know that girl can be a handful when you gone."

"That's why her father is gonna get her," Wayne said playfully as if he fucked Daffany, her real mother. "It'll give me a break."

Parade looked at him for a moment and hugged him tightly.

I sighed.

The last thing I needed was her Gay Husband interfering in our business because when the two of them were together the world was forgotten. They slid into the truck and my kids all hugged him. It was the most excited I heard them since all of this shit happened so for that I was relieved.

"Jay." Wayne said once he was seated in the third row with Landon.

"Wayne." I said. "So you just inviting yourself along for the ride, huh?"

"I'm inviting my friendship to help out friends." He said. "You see a problem with that?"

"Ain't no room at my mother's house for you." I let him know straight up.

"Nigga, please," he said waving the air. "The last place I'm gonna stay is with your spicy mother." He ran his index finger around the edge of his lips. "I'm Wayne. I'm worldwide. Trust me when I tell you I'll have a place to lay these legs."

Landon broke out into laughter.

I pulled off.

JAY

We had been driving four seven hours when I looked over at Parade who like everybody else was asleep. When she opened her eyes and yawned I smiled. "How you feel?" I asked. "You were out for awhile."

She rolled her eyes.

"Parade, you gonna be mad at me forever? We need —"

"I want a divorce."

I moved uneasily in my seat because I thought she said she wanted a divorce. "Can you repeat that?"

"You heard me."

My heart rate kicked up. "Parade, please, please don't leave me." I paused. "You not even giving me a chance to make shit right!"

She looked away.

I shook my head quickly. "Well I'm not letting you go," I continued. "On God, I'm not letting you break up our family. You know the nigga you married so I don't see why that should change."

"You did this to us," she whispered harshly. "Not me."

I laughed once. "Let's just get back to Maryland and talk about this like adults. Like a married couple. Because you and me know when I gave you that rock on your finger it was for life. And I'm not 'bout to let nothing break us apart. I'll kill somebody first."

She crossed her arms over her chest. "You can say what you want. All I know is I don't love you no more."

Suddenly my vision got blurred. It's like I could see the road in front of me but it looked like a bunch of fog was sitting on top of it. I rubbed my eyes roughly but it wouldn't clear up. Then my left arm started...it started...

"Jay, you okay?" Parade asked looking at me with wide eyes.

I looked over at her, wide eyed and...

CRASSSSSH!

CHAPTER SIX
PARADE

My sons were hugging me tightly on my left and right side as we stood. In the middle was Ella and she was holding my waist while Wayne grabbed my hand. We were standing in the middle of a private waiting room at the hospital in California waiting for the doctor to tell us what the status was on my husband.

Would he live or die?

Please God. Not like this.

Slowly the doctor walked up to us, his gaze not telling me anything. I broke away from my family. "Doctor…what…how is he?"

He took a deep breath and looked at my children and then at me. "Should we do this privately?"

"Tell us what's going on!" Wayne yelled.

"He's in a coma. Lost a lot of blood. He may not make it through tonight."

WEEKS LATER

WAYNE

"Danny, I know it's so sad," I sat back and looked over at Jay's mother's house. Parade and the kids were inside while I was talking to my husband on the phone. "At least he's stable now because at first...whoa. Things looked bad."

He sighed. "Well do they know what caused the heart attack? He's way too young to be having one."

"You telling me." I paused and took a deep breath. "Must be stress. Where is Shantay?"

"Out front with her friends."

"You can't let her do too much, Danny. You have to—"

"When you asked me to be her father I didn't agree to you telling me how to raise her too." He paused. "Now either you gonna accept how I'm doing things or—"

"I'm sorry." I put my fingers on my forehead and looked at my reflection in the rearview mirror. "That was wrong on my part and I'm...it's just that...I'm worried about both of you that's all. Jay possibly dying is too much and I guess I took it out on you."

"Just come home, Wayne. As soon as you can. I know Parade and Jay are going through their crisis but you have a family out here that loves and cares about you."

"SURE DO, BITCH!" Adrian yelled in the background.

"Sit down somewhere," Danny said to him before returning to our call. "Wayne, are you there?"

I laughed. "I'll be home as soon as I can."

"Make it quicker."

After I hung up with him I walked to the front door. Before I turned the knob I could hear Parade yelling at Melissa inside. The last violent confrontation they had consisted of Parade smacking Jay's mother to the floor and it didn't look like this would end any better.

Jesus, take the pen and write a way for us. Please.

I turned around when the front door opened. Wayne walked in and I was trying to regain my composure. Jay's mother was really working me and I was trying not to lay hands on her but I was on my last nerve.

"Melissa, all I want is for my kids to be okay until I figure things out." I said. "And I—"

"What about my son?" She yelled at me in her Spanish accent. "Huh?"

"You mean my husband?"

She moved closer. Thick wild black hair all over her sweaty face. "I heard about what you did to him." She pointed in my face. "How you broke his heart when all he wanted was to make things right." She placed her hands on her hips. "I heard what you said and how you treated him too. If my son dies…"

How could she know what was said in the truck? I looked at my daughter who was trembling across the room. I realized it was her who told her grandmother one thing too much. Her lips were gonna get her in trouble if she wasn't careful.

Melissa's words stung me like a hot blade and I felt myself choke on the inside, and then Wayne touched me from behind. He had a thing with appearing in my life when I least expected but always needed him. I considered him my living angel, despite not always agreeing with what he says.

When I looked around I saw Landon and Logan looking at me too. Their eyes begged for answers I didn't have. All day they wanted to know would their father be okay but I couldn't say for sure.

But Melissa was right about one thing. It was my fault. All Jay wanted was a chance to make things right and I denied him because of my pride. Had I just listened, had I just waited to hear what he said in the truck maybe we wouldn't be going through all this.

I took a deep breath and wiped my hands down my face. "Okay, Melissa, what you want from me right now? Huh? What can I do to keep the peace so we can focus on Jay?"

"I want for Jay to be better!" She yelled, spit flying from her mouth and plopping on everything near, including my arm. "But you can't fucking give me that now can you?" She moved closer.

"Mrs. Hernandez—"

"No! No!" She threw her hands up, palms in my direction. "You don't get to say shit to me. My son was sent to Maryland by Medevac all because you broke his heart. And I want you to know, just as sure as I'm standing in front of you, that I will never forgive you."

When Ella ran away crying I knew I would personally hate this bitch for the rest of my life.

I took another deep breath.

"I'm gonna put my family back together because you're right about one thing, this is my fault." I looked down. "And I will never forgive my own self until I—"

"Parade, don't—"

"Stop, Wayne." I looked back at him. "Just..." I took several breaths. "Just don't say anything." I focused back on Mrs. Hernandez. "And when I get my husband back on his feet let me be clear on one thing, you will never, ever, see us again. Trust me. I will tell him how you treated his family and he'll not like it one bit. You will pay for this shit."

"Don't fuck with me when it comes to my son you, black bitch."

"Now wait one fucking minute you—" I put my hand to Wayne's chest to stop him from unleashing on her.

"After all this time it's still about my complexion." I smiled. "Now we're really getting down to the heart of your heat. Your own grandkids, with the exception of Ella, have dark skin and look...you still being petty."

She crossed her arms over her chest. "I love my grandkids no matter what they look like. Don't make this about them."

I turned to walk away with Wayne following.

"Just know that my grandkids are always welcome here," she continued. "But it will cost you."

I turned to face her. "Excuse me?"

"Before you almost killed my child, me and Jay agreed to three hundred dollars a month in rent. I'm gonna be needing every penny payable in two days."

I shook my head. "Whatever."

"You greedy bitch," Wayne said under his breath.

He was right about that.

We walked out.

PARADE

"Parade, I know you feel like you gotta stay there but you don't," Wayne said as we sat in a diner in Bladensburg, MD, some place we both hadn't been in years. "His mother is way too disrespectful and the kids shouldn't be around that shit. At the very least let me take the kids back to L.A. so they can finish school and be with their friends."

"Ain't you paying attention? I already destroyed my husband. Now you want me to go against his wishes too?"

He took a deep breath and sat back, just as a waitress brought us two plates of fried chicken and rice.

"Parade, what…what *is* your plan?"

I sighed and grabbed my fork and scooped rice in my mouth. I knew he was fishing and I didn't want to have a long drawn out conversation with Wayne that I knew he wouldn't win. At the end of the day I would do things my way.

"Parade." He paused. "Answer me, girl."

"You know what I'm planning on doing."

He leaned forward, looked around and back at me. "Nah, I don't." He paused. "So make it clearer."

I sighed. "I gotta get my hands on $90,000 to get our house back and my business." I tore off a piece of chicken and ate it. "I mean if you got it that could save me a lot of time but at the end of the day I'ma do what I have to do. No matter what it is."

"You know if I had the money it would be yours, Parade. But with the money we spending on the restaurant, the surgeries and —"

"Wayne, I don't want your money." I reached over and touched his hand, squeezing it softly. "I just want you to understand what I'm going through and I want you not to judge my decisions." I paused. "To be honest even if you had it I wouldn't take it because I gotta do this my way."

"But..." He picked his fork up and dropped it back down. "But what does that mean? Because you dancing around and not answering my question. How you intend on scratching up all them stacks?"

"Wayne..." I looked at him. "You're a very intelligent young man."

"Oh, so you gonna fuck your way to ninety grand?" He said. "You got that much whoring in you?"

I shook my head. "After all these years you still the same judgmental ass nigga I knew from the Manor..."

"Nah." He pointed at me, which I hated. "The problem is so many people associate with fake people that they don't know a real friend when they see one. I'm not here to support your every decision if it will destroy you." He reached over and touched me. "And this will destroy you, Parade." He took a deep breath.

"You know how it feels to sit across from a friend that I have loved most of my life and say you're wrong, even if it means losing her?"

"I didn't ask you to come."

"Do you know how it fucking feels?" He slammed his hand on the table, his feminine voice replaced by his natural masculine tone. Something that always scared me when I heard it, which was rarely.

"Wayne, just —"

"No need to tell me to leave." He snatched his purse out the seat. "Miss Wayne knows when to make an exit, trust me."

He stormed away.

PARADE

"Well, it depends on what you want." I said to a man I met on *Play More Pay More*, a dating site that was really nothing more than a sex site. "And what you're willing to pay."

I flopped on the motel bed in the room Wayne was staying in before he temporarily moved in with a friend in Maryland, before going back to L.A. early after our argument. The room was paid up for a week so I decided to make use of it for privacy.

The terrible part was this, we only had a fight yesterday and already I missed him so much. But there was work to be done. I had to convince myself that I could be reckless in order to help the bigger picture.

I had to use my body.

What else was at my disposal?

Still, just thinking about it made my stomach turn and it bothered me beyond belief. When things got real bad, I thought about how Jay could still die and that if he lived I wanted him back in our house. Not with his mother who would probably tear us apart if we lived with her. That alone helped me make things easier. I don't care what I had to do.

"Well I want my dick sucked." He said right off the top. "And maybe fuck them titties or somethin' like that."

Disgusted, I hung up and tossed my phone on the bed. He sounded so vulgar and gross and that quickly I was starting to realize maybe I was making a mistake. But what was I going to do? Beg for hair clients online when I didn't have an online presence in Maryland? That would take more time than I had.

Or live with Jay's mother for life? Move with Wayne and anger Jay even more? My mother was dead. My father wasn't an option after recalling how he molested me as a child and even more how I accepted it.

What was left?

I had to use my body.

My cell phone rang. I picked it up off the bed and answered. "Ma."

It's Landon. "Hey, son. How — "

"Where are you, ma?" He paused. His voice sounded broken and sad and that made me want to break into tears. "What's going on? And why didn't you go with us to see pops today? Grams said you haven't been at all."

I took a deep breath. I hadn't been to see Jay since they flew him to the Maryland hospital. It hurt too much. "A lot is happening."

"Then explain it to me!" He yelled. "Because you're wherever you are and I need you here! With us!" He yelled and I could hear he was crying. "Did you hear me? I need you here with...me."

I placed my hand over my mouth to silence my own cries.

"Don't get me wrong, I care about Grandma," he continued. "Logan and Ella do too but she's not always nice."

I jumped up. "Is she hurting you?"

"No!"

I sat back down slowly.

"But, I don't like being around people who disrespect my mother."

I was so angry I trembled. "What is she saying this time?"

"It doesn't matter, ma." He paused "I just want us all to go back home, to L.A. where we can be together. Can you, I mean, can you do something about that?"

That was all the motivation I needed.

It was time to get to work and I was taking all callers.

CHAPTER SEVEN
PARADE

P arade walked into the small soul food restaurant that was closed for the night. Pete Chris, the overweight white and married owner, locked the door and licked his lips when he saw her enter. "The picture lied," he said as he observed her body and fished for his dick in his khaki's before grabbing it in his pants. "And for the first time I'm happy about that."

She sighed. "Thank you."

"Well it's true," he continued. "You're much sexier in person."

Parade looked down. The song and dance he was giving her was boring to say the least. She wanted to do her job as professionally as possible and bounce. "Where you want..." She looked at him. "You know...us to go?"

He pointed toward the back, his eyes filled with lust as he focused on her small breasts. "Follow me." He led her to the kitchen and toward the stainless steel worktable. They were definitely alone. "Right there. That's as good a place as any."

She looked at it and frowned. "But, isn't that used to prepare your meals?"

"Why you worried about it?" He paused. "You don't have a nasty disease do you?" He licked his lips. "Now take off your clothes."

She frowned. "Put the money in my app first." She pulled her phone out of her pocket.

He smiled. "I don't get to sample the goods?"

Irritated, she quickly walked toward the exit and he grabbed her hand softly. "Somebody's all about business." He removed his cell. "Just hope the pussy is as sweet as your game."

She gave him the information he needed to transfer the funds and when she received a notification that the money was in her account she placed her phone into her pocket. "Where you want me?"

"Waist down on the table." He unbuttoned his pants. "Ass up."

She complied. Slowly she placed her upper body on the table as he yanked down her black pants and eased behind her.

"Condom."

"I don't have any – "

She flicked one between her fingers. "Put it on or I'm leaving." She paused. "I told you that before I got here. And if you try something just know that I have somebody out there waiting to protect me," she lied.

He rolled his eyes, eased the condom out of the jacket and slid it on. As he entered her body she cried silently although he didn't know or care. She couldn't remember the last time another man touched her outside of Jay. Parade knew in her heart that her body belonged to her husband and yet there she was, allowing another person the honor.

Still, there was a reason.

She had zero money in her accounts because the banks took it all and the bills were mounting. There were no credit cards. No secret stash and no hope. And in that one foul act, less than ten minutes, she gained three hundred dollars, enough for Melissa's rent.

Her plan was simple.

Only deal with older men who could afford her up charge. So far married white men contacted her who had a craving for women with chocolate skin. And as long as they were paying she would be their fantasy but if she was being honest she couldn't see an end in sight for the ninety grand and yet she had to start somewhere.

PARADE

The second man she slept with was simple. He ordered her to lie down on her back in his daughter's bed as he entered her body. Things seemed normal until he pulled up to her ear and began yelling about how much he hated her calling her by a name she didn't know. And how ungrateful she was as his child. It was clear he had some secret hate-love-attraction to his daughter and that spooked her out.

His harsh words immediately brought tears to her eyes and for one moment in her mind she replaced his face and voice with Jay's. Since they were both Spanish the leap wasn't difficult to achieve. Being spoken too in a foul way was her way of taking the verbal abuse that she felt Jay had a right to inflict on her for causing the accident.

But things were about to get worse.

It had been three days and Parade managed to save up twenty five hundred dollars. She was exhausted when she made it to the motel for her next appointment. Her client was different than she normally dealt with because he was younger but he already paid a deposit of five hundred dollars with a promise to pay more once she got there and answered a few questions.

In all honesty she was hoping he'd say never mind which is why she asked for so much money. She was wiped out and wanted a day's break but he was willing to pay the vig.

Taking a deep breath she walked up to the door and sighed. When she was ready she knocked three times.

"It's open," a male's voice called out from the other side.

Parade pushed the door open and she was immediately shocked at what she saw. She saw his picture on the app but he looked much different.

Did he put up a false photo?

And if so why?

Her client was sitting on the bed, facing the door, hands clutched in front of him. What caught her off guard was how attractive he was. He definitely didn't look like a man who would be involved in buying whores. Then again, she didn't look like a whore either.

What she also noticed was the sudden surprise he appeared to have when he saw her. It was as if he'd met her before although they hadn't.

His locs, freshly twisted and tied, ran down his back. A goatee sat against his brown face and highlighted his smooth chocolate skin, sexy eyes and white teeth. Even though he *was wearing a white t-shirt, designer blue jeans and fresh black Nike boots. His demeanor said king.*

What shook her soul was that something about his presence, something about how he looked at her made her feel ashamed. As if he knew who she really was on the inside and was disappointed, despite the man never saying a word.

She closed the door and cleared her throat. It was her way to regain her composure. "The rest of my money please."

He grabbed his phone off the bed, pressed a few keys and she received a notification on her phone. When she pulled it out of her pocket she was surprised at the thousand dollars he deposited, eight hundred over their agreed amount.

"You do realize you gave me — "

He stood up. "On your knees, Lisa."

He used the fake name she gave him. "Wait, what — "

"I just paid you more," he said firmer. "So get the fuck on your knees."

She cleared her throat and slowly got down, before stuffing her phone into her pocket. After all he had paid more and successfully pushed her closer to the amount she needed to get their home back. Even if it was only a little closer.

"Now crawl."

She took a deep breath and moved slowly to him on hands and knees. Once she sat at his feet he looked down at her.

"So...um...so what now?" She asked, almost shaking.

He continued to stare.

"Um...so, what —" She cleared her throat. "What's next?"

Silence.

Tiring of being on her hands and knees she sat down and looked up at him. "What is this about? Huh? You paying all this money to look at me like you hate me? What's up with that? I mean what do you want to do?"

Silence.

She cleared her throat. "Listen, if you're going to be weird then..." She paused. "I'm leaving."

He continued to look down at her, hands clutched in front of him. For some reason when she looked at him she could feel a burning sensation above her cheeks and suddenly tears rose up in her eyes, before rolling down her face. The man had barely opened his mouth and yet something about his very essence had her weak.

Before she could stop herself she balled out crying and still he said nothing. It was so weird that she wasn't sure if he was even real. I mean, how was it possible for a man to be that silent and that overpowering?

Since he had yet to say more she got up and looked down at him. "Fuck you!" She yelled. "Do you hear me? Fuck you!"

He remained unmoved.

"I don't know what kind of game this is but I'm out." She turned to run out the door.

MERCER

Mercer sat on the toilet as his latest girl treat, Lanis, stood in front of him in the bathroom in the motel room. He removed her shirt about ten minutes ago, leaving her in her bra and jeans.

"Beautiful," He said gazing at her body.

She smiled. "Thank you, Mercer."

He unbuttoned her jeans and pushed them to her ankles. Placing his nose near her crotch, he inhaled deeply. Afterwards he frowned when he realized she wasn't wearing panties. "Why?" He asked.

"Why what?"

"You were out at the movies with me like this? It's a little whorish isn't it?"

She frowned. "Mercer, please stop the crazy shit or I'm gone."

Although disappointed in the lack of class, the last thing he wanted her to do was bounce. A serial killer for life, he wanted to kill her first. "Tell me you love me."

"You know how I feel about you," she said. "Stop with the games."

"I want to hear the words."

"I love you."

He smiled.

"Mercer," she continued. "You ask me that every time we're together. What happens if I don't say it?"

He ran the tub. "Get in." He paused. "I need to wash you."

RING. RING.

Mercer grabbed his cell phone off the sink. "Hello."

"Look, I need you to check out this female for me," Am'rak said.

"What's her name?"

"Just got her screen name, Lisa, and a pic." Am'rak paused. "But after I send it I need you to get on top of it ASAP."

CHAPTER EIGHT
PARADE

I could barely see as I walked down the street because tears continued to roll down my face. The worst part was I didn't know why.

Who was that nigga with his judgmental ass? And why would he pay $1,500 just to look down on me like I was some whore? I mean, I was doing whorish things, but, he didn't know my story. He knew nothing about me. And where is my fucking Uber?

It wasn't until I remembered that I told the driver to meet me in front of the motel that I realized I had walked five blocks away. He would never be able to find me down here. Since I was wearing heels my feet throbbed and I had to sit down for a minute to catch my breath before taking the hike back. And yet the entire time all I could think about was his screen name MRCEEREEYUS, which I now believed meant Mr. Serious.

When I spotted a stoop in front of a building I sat down and took off one of my heels to rub my foot. The moment I was seated a black beamer pulled up and parked on the street in front of me.

It was Mr. Serious.

My jaw dropped because he must've searched for me and I looked the other way. Why was he following me? Because there was no way I was having sex with him after how he treated me.

He rolled the passenger window down and leaned toward it. "You need a ride?" He asked.

His voice was deep and full of base. The kind of sound that went with a man who could make a grown woman cry without speaking. "I know you hear me over there," He said with a smile.

"Leave me alone."

"Listen, I'm sorry."

"For what?" I shrugged as I continued to look away from him. "You didn't touch me remember? So ain't nothing to be sorry for."

"Maybe that was the problem."

I glared at him. "What's that supposed to mean?"

He smiled.

Please, God. Get this man away from me.

I wanted him gone not for the reasons some may think. Yes he was attractive. Yes he smelled like expensive cologne when I entered the room. And yes he was younger than me, which meant he could probably make a person weak in bed if he wanted.

My reasons were simple.

I wanted him gone because I was a woman who was only in the position to sell myself to try and save my family. I didn't need no man or whatever he thought he was making me feel like shit.

"It means that if I would've done to you what I paid for maybe this wouldn't be happening." He paused. "You wouldn't be sad and I wouldn't be rolling up on some stalker type shit."

"Leave me alone."

"Nah," he smiled before looking in front of him and then back at me. "I can't do that."

"What does that mean?"

"You in the middle of nowhere at night." He sat back in the driver seat, head still in my direction. "The last thing I'm gonna do is leave you out here by yourself."

"I'm a grown woman."

"I know." He paused and picked up his phone. "I gotta make a few calls anyway so I don't mind waiting on your ride." He paused. "Wait, they are coming right?"

"What do you think?"

"I think we waiting on another nigga to do what I can...take you home." He paused. "If you ask me this is a waste of time."

I put my shoe back on and looked to my right and left for my ride. Although I knew he would never find me here. "This is so ridiculous," I said. "Just go away."

He smiled again and I heard him on the phone ordering pizza. When the call ended he said, "I put in a call for some food since —"

"What can I do to convince you to leave me alone? Because —"

"Let me take you where you going," he said. "Please." He paused. "I mean, technically you owe me since I dropped a band and a half on you." He rubbed his goatee. "That is, unless you not professional and into taking my money without the —"

I jumped up. "Don't say that. I may be many things these days but unprofessional is not one of them."

He smiled. "Are you sure about that cause..."

I crossed my arms over my chest.

He smiled again, leaned over and pushed the passenger door open. "What we waiting on?"

PARADE

I ended up at his house.

And I had a plan too. As easily as he put the money into my account something told me there was more where that came from. Could he spare ninety grand?

When I pulled up at his house in Upper Marlboro, Maryland I was shocked to see that his house was bigger than mine back in L.A.

He parked in a round driveway, walked around and opened my car door. There he stood, staring at me again. Not in a way that was mean or happy. Just in a way that made me feel awkward, like he knew something I didn't.

He extended his hand to help but I denied him, and eased out and around him.

He laughed. "You gonna do me like that huh?"

I crossed my arms over my chest.

"Follow me." He closed the car and I walked behind him up to his door. When we walked inside I wasn't impressed with the décor, because there wasn't any. Still, the place was beautiful. Chandeliers.

Cathedral ceilings. Spiral staircase. The works. But why was it so cold and empty?

"Haven't been here long?"

He smiled. "A year."

My eyebrows rose. "Doesn't look like you've done much decorating."

"Let's go upstairs."

I started to dispute but there was still the thing of him paying me for sex and me not giving him any. Plus for some reason I felt safe and not scared. That was a big problem too. I'm sure at least half of all murder victims let their guard down at some point.

Besides, I knew nothing about this person but something told me what he wanted from me was not sex related. Maybe Wayne being back in L.A. caused the wise part of me to be abandoned. Maybe I was foolish. All I knew was that I was about to see.

When we made it to the upper level there were many doors but we went to the first one on our right. The room was massive. Bigger than Jay's and mine and inside was a king sized bed, a table with two chairs and a large refrigerator and microwave. A red napkin dispenser sat in the middle of the table.

"You eat up here?"

"Hungry?" He asked ignoring my question, something he'd done a lot of.

I repaid him the favor by shrugging.

"Please," he pulled the chair out. "Sit down."

I swallowed the lump in my throat and took a seat. The thought of having to look into his eyes gave me extreme anxiety. He opened the refrigerator and pulled out a clear Tupperware container with a red top. He moved to the top of the microwave and placed two paper plates and two forks on the table. Next he opened the lid and scooped guacamole with lemon juice onto my plate. Finally he grabbed a box of organic pita chips off his dresser and sat down in front of me.

When he was done he grabbed a bottle of wine and a red cup and poured a lot inside. He sat it in front of me. "None for you?"

He shrugged. "Nah."

I smiled. "A man who doesn't drink," I said. "Different."

"Only the best for my body." He nodded. "Help yourself though."

What was up with him? I felt my heart rate elevating again. I ate the guacamole and chips and was surprised at how fresh and good it tasted. And then he looked at me. For a long time and I almost choked.

Wait...I was choking.

While I was coughing hard, he jumped up and hit my back lightly. A chip went flying out my mouth and I felt so dumb. "Are you okay?" He asked.

I nodded rapidly. A fist to my lips to cough a few more times.

He sat back down. "You have to be careful. I can't have you dying on me just yet. We—"

"What do you want from me?" I asked seriously. "I mean for real? What is your thing?"

He smiled.

"I'm serious," I continued.

He sat back. "Nothing."

"But this doesn't make sense. You paying more than the agreed amount. Choosing to stare me down instead of have sex. I mean, what are you...some college student doing a weird experiment on whores?"

"You not a whore." He paused. "And I'm not that young either."

"You younger than me." I said. "And anyway, how you know what I am?"

He reached across the table and grabbed my hand. Bringing it to his nose he inhaled. "Lavender on your skin. Not a pimple in sight. The tears that flowed down your face the moment you saw me, like immediately you had a reason for being there but regretted it." He shook his head. "I've seen whores and you not one of them."

I snatched my hand away.

"Yeah, you not a whore." He repeated. "Not submissive enough either."

I rolled my eyes. "Then what am I?"

"You're a woman in pain. And for some reason I want to know why."

"You don't know nothing about me."

"True."

"So what you talking about then?"

"I just made an observation, Lisa," he scooped a chip and guacamole before easing it into his mouth. "Am I wrong though?"

"Maybe I should call a—"

"I'm not a man who throws up what I do in people's faces." He leaned forward. "But I don't want you to leave and technically I did pay you too. Besides, I think we can be a benefit in each other's lives. If you give it a chance."

I crossed my arms over my chest. "Why you keep bringing the money up if you don't throw it up?"

He chuckled and put a hand over his heart. He dropped his hand. "It's just that I want you to stay.

And let me make a promise, I won't bring up that paper again if you do. Besides, it was short cash and meant nothing."

"Is that right?"

He wiped his mouth with a napkin. "Trust me."

PARADE

When I woke up I was looking at his sleeping face. All of my clothes were still on as well as his. It was at that time that I remembered it was because we didn't have sex. Didn't even hold each other. I also realized that I didn't know his name.

"Am'rak!" Someone yelled behind me. I quickly jumped off the bed and turned around, only to see a girl who looked so similar to me you would've thought we were twins. "Who the fuck is this?" She asked.

"I was just leaving." I searched for my shoes.

"You don't have to go nowhere," Am'rak said waking up. At least now I knew his name.

"This is not my thing," I grabbed my cell and shoes. The last thing I wanted was to get in a fight with a broad when I was married.

"So you choosing this bitch over me?" The girl continued to yell.

"Anja, why the fuck you up in my house tripping? Huh? I know you out there on your whoring shit again!" Am'rak yelled.

"I been stopped!" She responded.

"Your friends already told me," he continued. "Ain't no need in you lying. And how did you get in anyway?"

She dug into her pocket and removed a set of keys. "I see you don't know me at all." She tossed them at him. "Been made a copy. But you can take them or whatever if you want." She paused. "And yeah, I came over here because I heard you were trying to find me at work but now look…"

"I'm gone," I said to him. "And I'm sorry," I said to her. "But trust me, we didn't do nothing."

As I ran out the room and down the stairs I could hear them arguing. Now I think I knew what was happening. Am'rak was looking for her when he hit up the app and probably thought she was me. Later, one thing led to another and I was at his house.

For some reason I felt sorry for her because I know if Jay was with another woman I would be devastated. The good thing is that with me, she didn't have anything to worry about.

Not when it came to his heart anyway.

I was all about his cash because despite everything, he was the answer to my prayers.

I just knew it!

MERCER

When Mercer opened his eyes Lanis was looking at him. He rubbed his lids and yawned. "How long you been up?" He asked her with a grin.

"Where you from?"

He smiled. "You must want some more." He groped his dick.

"I'm serious."

He stared at her and yawned loudly. "Why?" He sat up.

"Just asking."

He glared. "Yeah, well you starting to move me wrong with all the questions."

She smiled. "Why though? I thought we were getting to know one another."

He frowned and stared at her for a long time. "Who sent you?"

She sat up. "Mercer, I — "

"Who sent you?" He yelled louder growing suspicious.

She stared at him and frowned before busting into laughter. "You know what, you a dumb ass crazy nigga. I knew you were weird when you bathed me but — "

Mercer removed the gun from his pillow and shot her square in the center of the head. The plan was always to kill her but he had hoped he'd get to keep her longer. His lifestyle didn't allow for a woman and once again he was reminded why.

Just then his phone rang. Wiping the blood from his face he answered, "Yes."

"Come get Anja out my house before I kill this bitch!" Am'rak snapped.

Mercer looked at the body next to him. "But I'm on a date and — "

"When I call you come." Am'rak paused. "That was the deal and there are no exceptions." He hung up.

Mercer sighed deeply and got out of bed.

CHAPTER NINE
LOGAN

"*So let me see your pussy then and stop faking,*" Logan said in the bathroom as he talked to his girlfriend on video chat.

Christy smiled. "You know I'm in class right?" She whispered.

He frowned. "Don't play with me."

"Okay, boy." She dropped the phone and put it under the desk. When her white panties were showing she pushed them to the side and unveiled what he wanted to see. When she was done she raised the phone again. "Satisfied now?"

He laughed. "I miss your ass." He pushed the thickness that grew in his pants to the right.

"Then come home." She said in a low voice. "What's taking you so long anyway?"

"I don't know what's up with my family," he shrugged. "I wish I did. But they keeping me and my brother and sister in the dark. To be honest I'm starting to hate them for real too." He paused. "Anyway, where your teacher?"

"She went to grab some new books from downstairs." She sighed. "Logan, you have to hurry up because I'm

getting lonely. Been thinking about getting a new boyfriend and – "

"Don't say that."

"Then what you want me to do? Be the only girl in school without a nigga?"

"Nah, but..." he took a deep breath. "Just give me a minute. I'ma get some money and I'm coming back to L.A."

"You promise?"

"Fuck you think?" He said seriously. "I'm not playing with – "

"Logan, what you doing in here?" Melissa said entering the bathroom without knocking.

"Grams!" He said ending the call and jumping up. "What if I was using the bathroom?"

"But you not using it." She paused. "Now clean your hands and come out here." She walked out.

When Melissa walked back into the living room, Parade was entering the house. She stomped up to Parade and placed her hands on her hips. "Where have you been?"

Parade laughed and walked around her and into the room she shared with Ella. "Where the kids?"

Melissa followed her. "Logon is in the bathroom doing God knows what and Landon and Ella went for breakfast up the street." She paused. "Now where were you all night?"

Parade pulled money out of her pocket that she earned from her work and handed it to her. "That's enough for another month of rent and groceries."

Melissa counted the money and tucked it into her pocket. "Ain't this something?" She said sarcastically. "You come in here smelling like a whore and — "

"Just so you know, I'm remembering everything you say to me. Verbatim. And when the time is right I'm gonna let my husband know just how foul you really are. When that happens I wonder what he'll think about you then." Parade yawned. "Now get out my face. I'm tired of looking at you."

Melissa rolled her eyes and walked out of the room.

"Logan!" Parade yelled before yawning again. "Come, come see me right quick."

"Give me a second," he responded back. "I'm in my room on the phone."

She shook her head. "Well hurry up." Still exhausted, Parade took a quick shower, put on some clean clothes and walked back into her room. Once inside she remembered she didn't tuck her money and pulled it out of her jeans on the chair before putting it under the bed.

Logan who was standing in the doorway saw it all. The moment she slipped into bed and went to sleep, Logan walked into the room, slid his hand under the mattress and removed the money, closing the door behind himself.

CHAPTER TEN
PARADE

I just walked out of Melissa's house after an hour nap. I spent a little time with my kids but I could tell they resented having to live with their grandmother. Logan on the other hand ignored me all together and I figured he hated me for taking him away from his girlfriend. Little did he know I was working on a plan to put us right back where we started.

I just needed to get the details together first.

I was about to walk to the curb in from of Melissa's house to catch a Lyft when Wayne pulled up in a rental car. I was so happy to see him a smile spread across my face before I remembered we were beefing.

So I crossed my arms tightly over my chest. "What you want, Wayne?"

"Oh, don't act like you don't live for me, bitch," he said. "Now get your ass in this car."

PARADE

We were at Fridays drinking martini's when I finally decided to ask him what I wanted to know. "So what made you come back?"

"I lost Daffany and Sky." He took a sip of his martini. "So, bitch, it's just me and you out here in these vicious ass streets. And although I don't agree with what you doing, if you gonna do it I at least want it to be done right."

I smiled. "Meaning?"

"You never gonna be able to fuck your way to ninety thousand, precious. You just won't. But you can seduce your way a little at a time *if* the mark is wealthy enough."

I smiled, picked up my drink and took a sip.

"What?" He said eyeing me closely. "Don't hold back. Spill that tea, honey."

I put my drink on the bar. "You must have a sixth sense for rich niggas because I definitely met one last night." I shook my head. "So your timing is impeccable."

BLACK AND THE UGLIEST

He frowned and didn't seem pleased.

"Why the sad face, Wayne? I just lent you a compliment."

"You just lent me a grin too. Now what else is up?"

I cleared my throat, trying not to appear guilty. "Oh."

"Parade, do I need to remind you that you a married woman?"

"No need." I waved my hand and took a deep breath. "I think about Jay every minute of the day. It's why I'm even thinking about this foul shit."

He looked at me suspiciously. "Mmmmm...hmmm."

"What?"

"The man must look like something because—"

"Okay, yes he's fine." I waved my hand. "Can't lie. But trust me the only thing on my mind is getting my husband out that hospital bed and kids out that woman's house and back into ours."

"I can get behind that."

"Good."

"So I guess you fucked him."

"Nope."

He smiled. "Perfect! Because that's exactly what we need you to do is hold off. If this man is rich and as handsome as you say he is, then its stands to reason that he is used to getting what he wants. Sooooo, we have to hold out on opening up your pockeybook to him as long as possible. Now at some point you may have to dish him up a plate of pussy but if we do things right by the time you do, you should be no more than five grand short of the 90,000."

I smiled. "So you really think I can, you know, get him to squeeze off that much cash?"

"You can get a man to do anything you want if your game is tight enough." He paused. "Remember that."

CHAPTER ELEVEN
JAY

*M*elissa sat at Jay's bedside clutching his hand. Every so often he'd breathe deeply and she'd smile, believing it was his way of communicating with her despite never regaining consciousness.

"I'm here, son," she said as she wiped tears streaming down her own face. "I want you to know that I'm here and I have someone on the way to see you. Someone you should've married instead of that whore. Someone who if you had made your wife would have never left your side."

Just then Quinn walked through the door. Mixed with black and Hawaiian, people who attempted to guess her ethnicity often failed miserably. When she saw Jay hooked up to the machines, she placed her designer purse on the available seat and hugged Melissa. "Mrs. Hernandez, I'm so sorry about — "

"Shhh," Melissa said as she pulled softly away from her and focused back on Jay. "I don't want any sadness around him. He needs strength and that means from you too."

"So what, what happened?" Quinn stuttered wiping her tears away. "I thought things were going good? I thought he was happy with his wife in L.A. and — "

"LIES!" Melissa took a deep breath and tried to hide the rage. "All lies apparently. Look at him! The last thing he is, is happy."

Quinn walked up to Jay and squeezed his hand while Melissa stood at his right. "But I don't want you worrying one bit, Melissa. I'm going to get him right." She smiled and leaned forward to kiss his cheek. "And when I do, he will be all mine."

Melissa grinned. "Now that's what I wanted to hear."

CHAPTER TWELVE
MISS WAYNE

Standing in the motel room I took a step back and gazed at Parade. She looked so sexy it made me proud. I couldn't believe I was doing this and yet here I was, helping my best friend cheat on her husband who was probably dying in the hospital as we speak. At the same time if she was going to fuck this nigga I wanted her to do it with my direction.

After we dressed her in a sexy one-piece black cat suit, red designer strap sandals and a blue jean Gucci jacket, I looked her over. From the front I could see that ass and I knew he would be pleased when he saw it too.

"Did he call yet?" I asked.

Parade nodded and took a deep breath.

"Good, remember whatever you do, you can't fuck this dude yet."

She rolled her eyes and flopped on the side of the bed before throwing her hands into her face.

Slowly I sat next to her. "What did I say wrong this time?"

She looked up at me. "Why is this my life?"

"You know you can't play this game with yourself anymore." I paused. "The whys won't change what's happening right now, Parade. Focus. Now we must do what we gotta to secure the bag. The only question is are you up for it?"

She nodded. "You know what..." She got up and stood against the wall across from me. "I'm afraid to see my own husband. Haven't laid eyes on him since he was flown here."

"I know. And that breaks my heart."

"Why do you think that is?"

"Guilt."

She nodded. "I think you right. Why else would I allow myself to stay away from the one man on earth I always wanted? I mean, even when Sky had him I knew he was for me, despite how he treated me. And now he's in a hospital and I'm about to do the worst thing ever. I hate myself and—"

I pointed at her. "I get it now."

She frowned.

"You want it both ways," I said crossing my arms over my chest. "You want me to bash you when you wanna be bashed about how you fucking over your husband and then cheer you on when it's time to get down to business."

"Oh, Wayne, cut it out," she said waving the air.

"I'm speaking gospel." I paused. "But I'm not gonna play your game. Now are you gonna do what you gotta do or not?"

She walked over to her purse, grabbed it and moved toward the door. With her back faced me she said, "You were always the one person who could see through my shit."

I laughed. "I don't see why that should change now do you?"

She laughed once and grabbed the doorknob. "I love you."

"Already know. Now get the fuck out and get that money."

PARADE

"So all of this is for me?" I asked Am'rak as I sat in his backyard where he had a chef prepare us a meal of lobster, mashed potatoes, asparagus and fresh bread under the moonlight. I also noticed a bottle of wine on the table with two glasses this time. Guess he was indulging after all.

He winked. "You impressed yet?"

"Nah." I grabbed my fork and ate some potatoes.

He laughed once and poured two glasses of wine, the one with the largest amount inside he gave to himself. "I guess you're used to this kind of thing right?"

I shrugged. "Not really." I lied. "But I thought you didn't drink."

He smiled, swallowed it all before pouring himself another. "I'm sorry about that situation when you stayed over the other night," He said ignoring me. "With my ex. Some women don't understand when its over."

"You sure that doesn't have anything to do with the games you play or the stories you telling her?"

He laughed harder. "You looking for the worst in me. Why is that?"

I shrugged. "To be honest I'm just here, enjoying a free meal. Looking for the worst in you is the furthest thing from my mind. Besides..." I ate some lobster. "Look how we met." I paused. "But you were looking for her weren't you? And you thought it was me when we met."

"Your photo was dark." He paused. "So the answer is yes." He pointed at me. "And that brings me to my next point. What were you doing there? You smell like a woman who's taken care of."

"I take care of myself."

"And I said I don't believe you."

"Maybe you're trying to make a story that won't sell. I'm a whore who was in need of money. You reached out and we connected. My story ends there."

"Exactly, but you couldn't go through with it."

"Was a bad day. We all have 'em."

"You remind me of my mother. Her life was snatched when somebody who was supposed to care about her failed." He glared at me hard, as if I were responsible. "And I'm gonna spend the rest of my life righting that wrong."

"And you think I can help you with that by favoring her?"

He smiled. "Can you?"

I bit my bottom lip, trying my best not to say the wrong thing because at the end of the day this was about the big money, the long con, and I had to be as Wayne said, engaged but distant at the same time. Wayne said I had to treat Am'rak the same way I did with Jay when we first got together, with one difference, I don't love this person.

"You think you are so—"

"I just saw some niggas around the house!" A man said rushing from the side of the house next to where we were. Suddenly four other men came around the back and I was about to shit myself until I realized they were with him.

Am'rak was calm as he stood up. "Check the perimeter and let me know what happens next," he told them. He walked over to me and softly placed a hand on my lower back. "Come with me."

"Is everything okay?" I could feel my heart thumping out my chest. I was trying to get a coin, not die trying.

"Hey, listen, I don't want you to worry okay?" He said to me. "You fine as long as you're on my side."

What did that mean?

I nodded and swallowed the lump in my throat as he escorted me into a dark house. When my vision was clearer, I saw men at every window and door. He led me upstairs and into his room, which was also dark, before closing and locking us inside.

"Am'rak, I...I..."

"Shhhh," he said as he pulled me to him. Afterwards he walked away, returned and handed me a gun. "It's a .45. Got one bullet. You know how to use it?"

I nodded yes and took it although I didn't. It had been so long since I fired a gun that I think I forgot on purpose. The piece he handed me was heavy and a revolver. I could feel the chamber and secretly hoped I wouldn't shoot myself instead.

Everything was happening so quickly. Every part of my being wanted to wiggle away from him but I needed to borrow his energy. I needed to borrow his calmness and…and for now my plan to get the money would have to take a backseat because I was scared for my life.

I sat on the bed and he walked to the window and moved the blind, which allowed the moonlight to shine inside. The only thing I could hear was my breath and still I didn't know what was going on.

He looked over at me. "Some dudes outside trying to get at me but my niggas on it okay?"

"Am'rak, I wanna go home."

"Yeah, well you can't right now." He said calmly. "Not because I don't want you to, but because it wouldn't be safe." His phone rang and he removed it from his pocket, looked at the screen and walked into the bathroom.

Afraid, and not knowing what to do, I got up and sat across the room, on the floor, away from the door. My chest moved up and down and all I could hope and pray was that I would get out of this situation alive.

With my knees pulled against my chest I watched the door closely. Every now and again I saw a shadow move by it from under the crack but for now no one came inside. Three minutes later the bathroom door opened and Am'rak came out.

"We have to go."

I stood up. "Where?"

"Some place safe."

"But why I gotta go too?" He paused. "Can't they just—"

"Your name is Parade Knight. And you lived around Quincy Manor."

Now I was rocked back to the floor where I looked up at his silhouette. I gave this man as little info about me as possible, so how did he know that much?

"I know a little about you," he said softly. "Now if I know a little about you that means they do too." He extended his hand. "So are you coming with me or would you prefer to die?"

CHAPTER THIRTEEN
MISS WAYNE

After sitting in my rental in front of Jay's mother's house for an hour, I decided it was time for me to face the music and go inside. Taking a deep breath I grabbed my purse and knocked on the door.

Melissa opened it with an attitude. "Fuck you want?"

"Maybe I should go back into my car, wait a few minutes and start over again."

She laughed. "You can do whatever you want and my response to you will be the same."

I shook my head. The old Wayne would've had her lips under his high heels but luckily for her I was a married woman with a husband, child and friends who loved me dearly. Still, I wasn't sure how much longer I'd be so gracious.

"Is Parade here or not?"

She folded her arms tightly over her chest and smirked.

"Fuck is so funny?" I asked.

"It's hilarious how you over here asking where she is when before she left she told her daughter that she was with you."

Oh, no, Wayne! How could you be so dumb? I thought.

"She was with me," I said trying to collect my fuck ups one by one. "But we got into it and she walked out my car a few minutes ago."

She shook her head. "You think you're soooo much smarter than me don't you? Think you have it all together. Well guess what, you don't. Now Parade may be captured by your feminine wiles but I'm not, and neither will my son when he wakes up and finds out what a bad mother your friend has been."

"You know what, I'm not gonna argue with you about all that." I looked over her shoulder. "Where the kids?"

Suddenly the smug look on her face disappeared. "Well, there's a problem with that too."

"Meaning?"

"Logan ain't here."

I put my hand over my chest. "What you mean?"

"He left and I've been calling his phone number but he won't talk to me."

"Well did he talk to Landon?"

She took a deep breath. "He won't tell me. But he's out right now with my nephew looking for his twin." She wiped her hand down her face. "I know they were staying here and all but I honestly believe Logan ran away because his mother wasn't here to handle her responsibilities."

I took one step closer so she could hear me clearly. "I have been respectful to you."

"You call the shit you said under your breath in my house the other day respectful? You think I didn't hear you? If anything—"

I placed a finger over her lips and pushed them closed. "Like I said, I have been respectful of you and your home. But if you say one more word about my friend in my presence or outside of it, and I find out about it, as God as my witness I will come back over here and stomp you to dust." I removed my finger. "Do I make myself clear?"

She backed away and slammed the door.

I removed my phone from my purse and made a call. "Honey, I need you to do me a favor." I paused. "Be on the look out for Logan. I think we got trouble."

CHAPTER FOURTEEN
PARADE

When I opened my eyes I was in the passenger seat of a Mercedes Benz. I knew it was new because it smelled that way. Am'rak was driving and he smiled at me as if everything was sweet. "You were out," he said, reaching out to touch my face. I backed away from him.

"Did you give me something?"

"Nah," he frowned, both hands on the steering wheel. I knew in that moment he did. "Just the juice you asked for."

I rubbed my head. "Well how come...I..."

"You hungry?"

My mouth was dry and my stomach rumbled before I could respond. It would be dumb to lie at this point or let on that I was scared even though I was. The last thing I remembered was being in his house and now...now I don't know where we were. "I can eat," I said. "Actually I'm starving."

He smiled. "I know the perfect spot."

I looked out the window. There was a black Mercedes Sprinter in the front and back of us so I knew we were driving in a caravan.

Dear God, please get me out of this safe and unharmed.

"Are they following us?" I asked. "The vans in the front and back of us."

"I always have my important people and packages followed." He replied.

"Well, where, where are we?" I asked. "And what's going on?"

"We're in Virginia." He paused. "The deep south part. That's all you need to know for now."

My eyes widened. "But I...I can't be here...I have to...I gotta..."

"You gotta what?" He paused. "I mean, you said you don't have kids or a man, Parade. So what you gotta do that's more important than saving your own life?" He looked at me and then back at the road.

"Am'rak, I—"

"If I pull this car over and let you out there would be no less than thirty niggas that I can think of prepared to take your life. All 'cause they think you important enough to me since I brought you to my house. Is that what you want?"

"Brought me in your house?"

"Yeah." He nodded. "Outside of my ex I don't bring people to where I live."

I rubbed my eyes and tried to stop the heavy breath from rising and falling in my chest but it was difficult. "Where are we going to eat?" I wanted my mind off of everything else.

"We gonna go by my crib which is a few miles up and then I'll order out." He placed a hand on my thigh and rubbed it softly. My skin crawled. "And I don't want you to worry. As long as you with me you're safe."

When his cell phone rang he answered. I couldn't hear the caller but I could tell his demeanor was softer when he saw the number. It was almost child-like. "Don't worry about it," he said into the phone. "I know you can't go through it again." He looked at me. "And you won't have to either." He paused. "But I gotta go. I'll call you back."

Was that the girl who walked in on us at his house?

Did she know I was with him now?

There were so many questions and not enough answers!

PARADE

This house was as big as the one in Maryland if not bigger. It was also just as empty, which had me wondering what exactly did he do for a living. Why all the fucking houses not furnished? I mean I knew it was drug related, at least I thought so, but I didn't know how deep he was into the game and if he was more hated than loved.

"Where is your bathroom?" I asked when we walked into the living room.

"Use the one upstairs."

I smiled, gripped my purse tighter and walked upstairs. Once there I closed and locked the door and sat on the closed toilet seat. When I rummaged through my purse I noticed my phone was gone and my heart thumped harder. Leaping up, I paced in circles and placed my hand over my chest. Why did he take my phone? This shit was getting more and more out of hand and I was now officially in fear for my life.

"Okay, okay, Parade you have to calm down." I said to myself. "First off you don't know what's going

BLACK AND THE UGLIEST

on. Yes you appear to be taken by a man who is dangerous and hunted. And yes you have no idea where you are. But if you don't get it together..."

A few tears rolled down my face during my self-talk and I took a deep breath and wiped them away.

"...If you don't get yourself together you're probably gonna make things worse. Now go out there and be on your game."

I walked over to the mirror and turned on the water. There were tiny spider webs around the designer faucets and I knew he hadn't been here in a while. After throwing cold water on my face I took another deep breath, flushed the toilet and walked downstairs.

Before I turned the corner I saw Am'rak talking quietly with two of his men. They all looked at me and Am'rak dapped them up and they walked off, leaving us alone. He smiled, extended his hand and walked me to the kitchen where two paper bags filled with food sat on top. "Sit down."

"That was quick," I smiled pulling up a wooden chair, one of four at a table that matched. "You had somebody bring food that fast?"

He sat across from me and removed a Styrofoam plate filled with pancakes, eggs, potatoes and sausage for both of us. Then he removed two cups filled with orange juice.

After handing me a fork he said, "I had to take your phone. I'm sorry."

"My phone?" I frowned as if I didn't know already. "I didn't even realize it was gone." I ate some eggs, which were beyond good at this point. Or maybe it was the fact that I was starving and horrified at the same time.

He smiled. "It's just that, you know, with niggas chasing me I gotta be careful. Don't want people knowing where I am. I tried to get into it to turn off your location finder if you had one but couldn't because I didn't have your code. Since you had a Samsung and not an iPhone I couldn't even use your fingerprint to unlock it. So I had to toss it out the window on the highway. I hope you can understand."

I nodded. "Um, I am confused though." I kept my eyes on my food as I put bits and pieces into my mouth. "I mean…"

"My best friend is doing this shit." He said answering my question before I asked.

I put my fork down and wiped my mouth. "Your—"

"We grew up together. Made a lot of money together and he, and he stabbed me in the back. Now he wants me dead and out the way and I'm not gonna let that happen."

I nodded my head although I didn't believe him. Everything in me wanted to ask more questions but Wayne kept telling me how important it was not to look too desperate. And so far it seemed to work because he was talking to me freely without me asking specific questions. Still, what could cause a man to hunt his own best friend if that were true?

I picked my fork up and ate some more eggs.

I could feel him judging me and trying to figure me out with his eyes. "You not gonna ask me anything else?"

I took the lid off my juice and took a large gulp. "Do you want me to ask you something else?"

He laughed hard.

"What?" I put the cup down and tore off a piece of pancake. I don't even think I was hungry anymore. Just trying to do something to appear relaxed even though it was the furthest emotion from my mind. "Why you looking at me like that?"

"We gotta stay here for a few days, maybe a week or so, but I want things to be good for you."

I swallowed the lump in my throat. "Am'rak, that's a long time to be away from my life."

"I thought you didn't have any place to—"

"Just because I don't have a family and, you know a..."

"A man," he said finishing my sentence. "You single right, Parade?"

"Just because I don't have a boyfriend and kids doesn't mean I can stay posted up here with you for weeks. I mean, that's not how you do people."

He nodded and sat back in his chair. "I'm not holding you hostage." He wiped his mouth with the napkin and then pointed at the door. "You free to go."

I looked toward the living room and back at him. "And then what?"

"What you asking? If you'll be safe or not?"

Silence.

"Like I told you in the car I can't call it," he shrugged. "I mean, I told you why you here. Now if you think you can make it on your own and stay clear of Salaam then go for it."

I looked down at the plate and back at him. "I need to make a call."

He smiled. "Let me get you a clean phone."

AM RAK

I haven't heard anything else from my contact," Mercer said while he was on the phone with Am'rak who was in the basement of the house in Virginia. "So far the FEDS still looking for Quila, not you."

"If I gotta give 'em my name instead of hers I will but —"

"Hold off on that," Mercer said. "We just have to find another scapegoat. If they want a plug, lets give them one."

Am'rak sighed. "What about the girl? Any more info on her?"

"She moved to L.A. some time back and that's all I got so far."

"Well don't stop looking," Am'rak said. "She may be the answer to my prayers."

When he hung up with Mercer he called his aunt. "Hey."

"What's going on?" She said anxiously. As the drug dealer known as Queen Pin, she was wanted by many although few ever seen her face. At 77, she was also getting old and senile. "Are they on to me or what?"

"I don't want you to – "

"I can't do the time, Am'rak," she said hysterically. "I just can't. You know that right?"

"Hey, hey, hey," he said firmly. "I'm going to always take care of you and I want you to know this time won't be any different. I don't care who I have to kill!"

PARADE

I was standing in the middle of the living room using a phone that Am'rak gave me while he was in front of the house talking quietly with his men again. There was always so much secrecy around him that it was another reason why I wondered how I didn't zap the fuck out.

When the phone rang for the fifteenth time and still no Wayne, I was starting to get nervous. He always answered when I called. FUCK! I just needed him to know what was happening in the event I was missing for good. "Aw, Wayne, please, pick up. Where are you?"

MERCER

Mercer sat in his car in the parking lot of the hospital looking at Quinn who had just left visiting Jay, who was still unconscious. When she unlocked the car alarm to her silver Range Rover, she felt as if someone was watching.

She was right.

When she turned around she saw Mercer in his car staring intently. But instead of being fearful she smiled. After all, he was handsome with his smooth brown skin and big eyes.

He smiled back.

The move, although simple melted his heart. Who was she?

He continued to watch her until she pulled away and immediately his heart told him he loved her and he was determined to make sure she loved him back.

When the phone rang he answered. "Any word?" Am'rak asked.

Mercer cleared his throat. "Still running short but I think I found her mother."

"Really?"

"Yeah. A friend of mine said he heard Parade arguing with a Latin broad in the parking lot of the hospital some time back. Said the broad was mad that Parade wouldn't go inside. He thinks she's her moms."

"Sounds off based on the description."

"I know," Mercer admitted. "The picture you sent doesn't say Latin but she could be her foster moms or something. Who knows?"

"Maybe," Am'rak said slowly, not really buying it. "But keep digging. I feel like we're close."

"Can you tell me why she's so important?"

"Just do what the fuck I said," he snapped before hanging up.

CHAPTER FIFTEEN
WAYNE

I was standing in front of Janson High School in Maryland when I finally saw Landon walking out talking to another young boy. They were laughing at something until Landon saw me. He said a few words to the boy and walked over to me.

Sliding into the rental he hugged me and took a deep breath. "Before you ask I don't know where Logan is."

I stared at him harder.

"I know you don't believe me." He took a deep breath and continued. "But he wouldn't tell me where he was going either so…"

I continued to stare as he looked out the window, anyplace but at me.

Finally he took a deep breath. "He went back home, Wayne."

I shook my head. "I knew it." I paused. "How on earth did he get there?"

"His girlfriend arranged a ride for him from a friend who was in the area I think." He shrugged. "It was gonna take them a few days to get there driving but he had some cash on him before he left. Don't know where he got it." He shrugged. "I'm sorry for lying to you, Uncle Wayne."

I took a deep breath. "Don't worry about all that." I paused. "We will—" When my phone rung again with an unknown number I looked down at it and frowned. I didn't wanna talk to anybody unless it was Parade so that meant keeping the line clear. After realizing it wasn't her number I put it back down and looked over at him. "Okay, this is what we gonna do, I don't want you saying anything to your grandmother at all about this. And the moment Logan gets to L.A., the first person you going to call when you hear from him is me." I sighed deeply. "I don't want your mother worrying about this before she has to."

He nodded. "Okay."

I looked over at him again. "How are you though?"

"Fine I guess."

"Landon," I said softly. "You have always been the level headed one in this family."

He laughed. "I know and that's scary considering how stressed I am."

"You'll learn to appreciate it later in life when you need to draw on that strength." I paused. "And I know how that is, having to always come to the rescue and help others. But I truly want to know how you feel and to tell you things will be okay. Trust me and trust—"

"Please don't lie to me." He said. "You never lied to me and I don't want that to change."

I nodded my head softly. "You're right." I paused. "This situation is a disaster. But I believe in my heart that something will work out for this family. It just has to."

When the nurse walked into the room to sponge bathe Jay, Quinn stood up and walked toward her. "Hello, I'm his wife," she lied.

The nurse nodded. "Yes, his mother told me." She looked at Jay and back at her. "I'm just going to bathe him and — "

Quinn blocked her path and removed the bucket with warm water and sponge floating inside, from the woman's hands. "You can leave now. I have this. I don't mind."

"But I'm supposed to — "

"The door." Quinn placed the bucket on the table next to the bed. "Now."

The nurse smiled, nodded once and walked out.

Quinn closed the door, walked over to Jay and pulled the covers back. Next she raised his baby blue hospital gown. Looking at his body with eyes that should not cover a man who was not hers, she observed each inch of his unconsciousness. His chiseled biceps, six pack and flaccid but well-hung dick all had her licking her lips.

"Wow, better than I remember," she said to herself.

When she was ready she touched his body carefully. Slowly her fingertips trickled over his forehead, nose, cheeks and lips. When she was excitable enough she did the same to his neck, chest and belly. And as if that wasn't too much, she touched his limp penis, thighs and feet.

She would've done more but she heard someone else walk by the door talking and didn't want to be caught in such an awkward position, heaven forbid it was Jay's mother.

So, dipping her hand into the warm water, she grabbed the sponge and wiped his face while staring down at him with penetrating eyes. "You will be mine this time, Jay. And there won't be anything anyone can do to stop it. Especially your fucking wife."

PARADE

I hadn't even realized I was asleep until I opened my eyes. Pushing the thick and stiff silver comforter and sheet set off me, I sat on the edge of the bed. The cat suit I was wearing was too tight and uncomfortable, causing me to wake up several times during my nap making me unable to get the good rest that I desperately needed.

There was so much that needed to happen in my life, starting with me talking to my family and finding out what was up with Jay but I had no such luck. I didn't know Melissa's number. My sons weren't answering their cell phones and Wayne wouldn't pick up his either.

What was going on in my family?

Walking out the bedroom I headed downstairs, only to see Am'rak sitting on the sofa, with three large red boxes on top of a cream-colored living room table that wasn't there before. He looked drunk and angry which made me pause.

"Are you okay?" I asked softly.

"Was life always easy for you?"

I laughed.

"Answer the question." He glared.

"Not even close."

"Why don't I believe you?"

"Am'rak, what is this about?"

He stood up and put his arms behind him. "Let's play a game."

I walked closer and looked down at the gifts. "Is this for me?"

"You playing or not?" He asked with a smile.

"I actually wanted to try and reach my friend again." I looked in the kitchen where I put the burner on the charger. "Is the phone charged up now?"

"My man's using it," he said softly. "But what about the game? Are you willing to play?"

I took a deep breath and crossed my arms over my chest. "What's in it for you?"

He laughed. "Shouldn't I be asking you that question?"

I shrugged. "Okay...what's in it for me?"

"You pick one of the boxes and you get to keep anything that's inside."

I looked up at him and walked on the other side of the table. Taking a deep breath I sat down and stared

BLACK AND THE UGLIEST

up at him again. He was getting weirder and weirder by the day. I mean, did he like me or hate me? "I don't get it, Am'rak."

He sat next to me. "I'm guessing that you are intending on staying here with me a little while correct?"

I shrugged. To be honest I wanted to go home but was afraid of getting the bullet in the head that he told me repeatedly I would receive from his enemies. "Uh, yeah." I cleared my throat. "Yes."

"Well if you are," he continued, "The least we can do is have fun."

"Okay, if I pick the box in the middle —"

"Just choose," he said firmly.

I moved uneasily because he sort of snapped. The weight of my choice appeared heavy. "Is this supposed to be fun because it feels real scary?"

"I'm sorry," he said. "I just don't want you messing up a good thing. You'll learn to look back on this moment with regret if you aren't careful."

I took a deep breath and grabbed the smallest box. Looking at him out of the corner of my eyes I saw him smile. The box was flat and no bigger than the palm of my hand but I was hoping that it was money. When I opened it there was a small gold envelope inside that felt like a credit card.

Slowly I pulled back the lid and saw a white card with the words "Te concedo un deseo".

He smiled. "You picked the best one." I didn't feel that way. "Give it to the one person in your life who you love the most. It'll be very useful. Trust me."

"But what does it mean?"

He winked and there was a knock at the door. "I'll be back."

"Can I use your phone now?"

He smiled, dug into his pocket and handed me a black flip phone. When he walked to the front door I made a call and finally Wayne answered. I was so shocked to hear his voice I got choked up. "Wa...Wayne...you...what...how..."

"Parade?" He said hysterically. "Is that you?"

"Yes, where...why didn't you answer your phone?" I got up and walked to the kitchen for a little more privacy. "I been calling you all day. Nonstop."

"Chile, I didn't recognize the number!" He said frantically. "Where are you?"

"It's too much to say but I have to know what's going on with the kids. Are they fine?"

He took a deep breath.

"Wayne?" I repeated, wild eyes darting around. "Are my kids okay?"

He took another deep breath. "Okay, well, Logan has gone back to L.A."

I placed my hand over my chest, leaned against the wall and slid down to the floor. It took everything in me not to scream. "But, but..."

"He got some money from somewhere."

It was then that I remembered that I tucked some cash under the bed at Melissa's and he must've found it.

"But Parade, I don't want you worrying about anything." He continued. "You know I won't have my nephew rolling around L.A. without my involvment. Trust me. He'll be safe." He paused. "But where are you?"

"I have no idea," I sniffled, wiping the tears that crept up on my face. "One minute I was at his house in Maryland and the next minute some dudes had broken in and he moved me out of state. I—"

"WHAT?"

"As ridiculous as it sounds, is as ridiciulous as things have been over here." I paused. "I mean, at one point I thought he was holding me hostage but I don't think that's the case."

"Parade, maybe you should go home." He paused. "I had a bad feeling before but now..."

"I can't come home just yet," I said standing up. "I've come too far you know? And if I don't at least try to get the money then what am I doing? What has all this been about?"

"Who you talking to?" Am'rak asked walking into the kitchen.

"Let me call you back." I hung up on Wayne. "A friend of mine." I walked over to him. "Is everything okay?"

He stared at me for a few seconds. "The phone." He extended his hand.

"What?"

"The burner." He stepped closer. "Give it to me."

"Oh." I handed it to him although I didn't want to. Origianlly the plan was to delete Wayne's number but now he had it before I could.

"I just found out we may be able to leave in two days." He tucked the phone in his pocket. "You think you can stand being around me that long?"

"Yeah, I mean, what can happen in a few days?"

BLACK AND THE **UGLIEST**

CHAPTER SIXTEEN
LOGAN

*L*ogan sat on the porch at his girlfriend's house with her while eating Jack In The Box cheeseburgers and fries as if everything was sweet. When she was done she looked over at him and said, "Can I have your fries too? Mine gone."

He smiled. "You can have anything you want."

Christy grinned and kissed his cheek. "Nah, I don't want 'em. Just wanted to see if you would give 'em to me. But I'ma give you something in a second." She covered her mouth and laughed. "Just as soon as my dad goes to sleep."

"Why you do that?" He asked placing the rest of his burger in his bag.

"Do what?"

"Cover your smile?"

She shrugged. "Didn't know I was doing it I guess."

"Yeah, you do," he paused. "A lot too." He took a deep breath. "My mother does it sometimes too but...you know what, fuck that bitch."

"Whoa."

"That's just how I feel about her right now." He clutched his hands together and sighed while looking at the block. "How you just gonna leave your kids and husband in a hospital to die? It's like she couldn't wait to be in the streets or something."

Christy sighed. "I'm not gonna fake like I like your mother 'cause you know we stay going at it because she doesn't want us together. But I know for a fact your mother loves you."

He looked at her for a moment. "Is that why you pressed me out to come back? 'Cause you love my moms so much?"

"Nah." She paused. "I just wanted you with me. I know that's fucked up but even still I know your mother..." Suddenly her attention was drawn up the block. "Hold up, ain't that your mother's friend?" Christy pointed in the direction she was gazing.

The moment Logan saw Adrian stomping down the street wearing a black bob, blue jeans and a tight white t-shirt he knew it wouldn't be an ordinary day. When he was up on him he said, "Get up, boy." Adrian paused. "You coming with me."

Logan rolled his eyes. It wasn't in his makeup to be disrespectful to his mother's friends but he didn't come that far to leave Christy and go back to Maryland either. Plus he didn't want to look dumb in front of his girl. "I'm not going nowhere."

Adrian covered his heart with one hand and the other with his mouth. "What you just say?" He asked through his fingertips.

"I said I'm not goin' nowhere."

Adrian dropped his hands and nodded slowly. "I'm gonna give you an opportunity to take that back and come with me now. But you'll only get one chance."

Logan looked at Christy and back at Adrian. "I'm not going anywhere."

Adrian smiled, turned around and walked slowly up the block with Logan watching him every step of the way.

"What you think he gonna do?" Christy asked.

"I don't know." He shrugged as he continued to eye him. "Maybe tell my moms if he can find her." He pulled her to him and kissed her lips. "What do I care? I'm not leaving you."

"I don't know about this," she swallowed the lump in her throat. "The look in his eyes seemed scary to me."

"I don't care what he does." He paused. "I'm staying here."

PARADE

It was pitch black in the bedroom of the house we were staying in and I had a bad dream. I was so scared that had Am'rak been in the bed with me I would've grabbed him for protection. But he hadn't said two words to me since he took the phone after I got off it with Wayne. And so I was left alone, wondering if he would hurt me for whatever reason.

Anyway, I dreamt that Jay had died and had been reincarnated into a new family. At first I wasn't worried that he died because at least he was alive. I even followed him in my dream but when I walked up to him he didn't recognize our kids or me. It was so weird the pillow was wet because obviously I had been crying.

Sitting up in the room, I was surprised when I saw a black cell phone on the dresser across from the bed. I walked toward it, turned the lamp on and made a call.

"Wayne, it's me, did you find Logan?" I whispered, looking at the closed door to be sure Am'rak wasn't coming.

BLACK AND THE UGLIEST

"Yes, girl. You know I did."

I wiped my hand down my face in relief. "He's with *her* right?"

"Chile, what you think?"

I tried my best not to cry but nothing was going right in my life. With my world being a disaster. It was like I was reverted back to the Quincy Manor days and I wondered why. What part of the lessons I learned did I actually fail and have to retake? I didn't understand.

"Don't worry, Parade. I'm going to get him back. Trust me."

"He won't leave with anybody you send."

"Oh, baby, he won't have a choice." He paused. "Listen, I want you to know that I'm handling everything I can on this end. And I want you to know that I'm tough enough for it too, which is why I left L.A. to be with you. But all I want is for you to meet me half way, get that money from that nigga and come home. As soon as—"

I heard bumping outside the room that caused me to put the phone down. When it seemed like the coast was clear I placed it back against my ear. "Wayne, I gotta call you back."

"Make sure you do," he said. "Because now you have me worried."

"I will. Just please bring Logan back."

I ended the call, erased the number out of the phone and walked out the room. The lights were all out in the house. For some reason Am'rak liked to keep it dark and that always made me uneasy. Who was he hiding from now? Luckily there was a small night light on next to the far corner of the living room and I could see two men standing over another who was moaning quietly on the floor. The two men standing up were talking to each other and when the man on the floor tried to move one of them kicked him in the face.

I covered my mouth.

I almost cried out when a hand came down over my lips. Within seconds I was dragged back into the mostly dark bedroom only to see Am'rak looking at me. "Tomorrow I can take you home. The nightmare is over."

I exhaled, placed my hand on my chest and flopped down on the edge of the bed. It wasn't until that moment that I realized how badly I was scared about everything, even my own shadow. "Thank…thank you."

He sat next to me. "You probably never wanna see me again do you?"

I looked up at him and thought about the ninety grand I still needed. Thanks to the moonlight coming inside I was able to see some of his features. "I don't know what I want right now." My thoughts moved to what Wayne said about not saying a lot and I bit my tongue despite wanting to know what was happening downstairs.

"What you saw was necessary." He said softly. "And I know all of this has been hard for you but to be honest I'm happy I had this chance to get to know you. This time together put you in a new light for me. And if you never want to see me again, I just want you to know I'm here."

The door opened and a man dressed in a black hoodie and black sweatpants walked into the room. "We ready for you."

Am'rak looked down at me. "Chill in here until I come back." He placed his hand on the side of my face. "It's almost over." He winked and walked out with the dude.

LOGAN

Under Christy's bed, Logan looked at the bedroom door waiting for her to come back. She had been gone for three hours and although he wanted to be with her he wondered how much longer would he have to fake like he wasn't tired.

He was about to say fuck it and slide out when she entered.

Carrying a plate of mac and cheese, fried chicken and biscuits, he slid from up under the bed to eat. Sitting on the edge of her mattress he took the plate and kissed her. "Thanks, bae."

"Sorry it took so long." She sighed. "My father all of a sudden wanted to talk about school and shit. It's like he knows something is up. He never, ever talks about my life."

Logan took a large bite of chicken. "Yeah, well your mother knows how to cook."

She shrugged. "That was my dad actually." She paused. "My mother she's, well, she's hardly ever here. I will give my father that much. He cares enough to check on me."

He looked into her eyes. "I get that. My mother always at the shop too and then wonders why I don't fuck with her.

It's like I don't know who she is anymore. All she wants to do is talk about work and how much she's sacrificing and now look." He paused. "We don't have none of that shit. No house or nothing. I'm out here sleeping under my girl's bed and she — "

Suddenly loud music sounded outside of Christy's house. Noisy and ratchet trap music, way too much for the quiet 10:00 PM hour of the neighborhood, rocked both of them to the core. Horrified, Christy leapt up and looked out the window. "What is...what's going on?" She asked.

Logan sat the plate on the bed and walked over to the window. He peeked out and what he saw, caused his stomach to churn. Adrian was standing on top of a car dancing in little tight blue jean shorts and a white t-shirt that was tied up in the back. Two of his equally feminine male friends had their hands on the car and asses in the direction of Christy's house as they popped their fat cheeks.

"Wait, ain't that your — "

"I gotta go." He lifted the window and climbed out as quickly as he could, scratching his knees in the process.

"Please don't leave," she said placing her hand on his. "You all I have."

He grabbed the back of her head, kissed her lips and smiled. "I promise. I'll be back soon."

He jumped down from the window and walked up to Adrian. Without saying anything he opened the back door and slid inside the car. Adrian got in the driver's seat and his friends piled in the right and left side of him before pulling off.

Adrian looked at Logan from the rearview mirror. "I know you angry but your mother is loved. And that makes you loved too."

He rolled his eyes. "Yeah, whatever," he said, trying to hide the smile creeping up on his face.

CHAPTER SEVENTEEN
PARADE

I had just finished taking the meatloaf out of the oven when I heard the front door open. Landon and Ella were already at the table and both were happy to see me. But it was Logan who I was concerned about and I had a feeling it was him walking in the front door.

When I walked toward it and saw Wayne behind my son I was right and breathed a sigh of relief. Logan's arms were crossed tightly across his chest and his expression was away from me.

"Logan," I said softly. "I'm glad you're back."

"I just picked him up from the airport," Wayne said. "I'm gonna leave you to it. Danny's on the phone and we...well, let's just say it ain't good. We'll talk later though."

Before he walked out I ran up to him and hugged him tightly. Wayne hugged me back and left. I swear I don't know what I would do without him and I was never trying to find out.

When the door was closed I walked over to Logan. "Hungry?"

He rolled his eyes and stomped into the kitchen where he hugged his little sister and dapped up his brother. Next he sat down at the table and looked at me. "You got me here now what?" He looked around. "And where Grams?"

"She been staying by the hospital," Landon said. "To keep an eye on Pops."

Logan nodded.

I sat down at the table and looked at my children. "I know I haven't been the mother I'm supposed to be. But I promise you all this," I looked at them. "I will get us out of this house and back into our home."

"How though?" Logan snapped. "I mean, you got us in Maryland and now you saying you can put us back into the house? How when you broke as fuck?"

"Just like I got that money you stole from me, is the same way I'm gonna make it happen."

He sighed. "Yeah, whatever."

"Son, there are a lot of things you don't know about me. And there are even more things that I'm willing to do to keep my family together. Just know that if I say we will be back in L.A. that's exactly what I mean. Just please, please don't run away again."

"So what you gonna do?" Logan continued. "Whore yourself out?"

He was so close to the truth I rose up and slapped him.

He stared at me and ran to his room. It was the first time I'd ever hit one of my kids. "Logan!" I yelled. "I'm sorry!"

I walked toward the door but Landon grabbed my hand, stopping me. "I'll keep an eye on him, ma." He said softly. "Just, just do what you say you gonna do. Please."

I hugged him and then touched Ella's face. Grabbing my purse I looked back at Landon and said, "Make sure everyone eats."

"Where you going, mama?" She asked me.

"To work on getting us out of here." I said with certainty. "But first I'm gonna go see your father. It's time."

MELISSA

Melissa and Quinn sat in Jay's room laughing about how Jay and Quinn met in high school, long before Sky came into the picture and long before he met Parade. Quinn was playing in P.E. class with her boyfriend when Jay came out of nowhere and hit the dude in the jaw and walked out. There were no reasons given and everybody wondered why he embarrassed him so badly in front of his girl.

For weeks Quinn would approach Jay and ask why he assaulted her boyfriend who was too afraid to be with her anymore after the hit, thinking she was the reason. And each time she would ask, Jay would smile at her and walk away. It wasn't until she was about to leave to stay with her aunt in Florida that he finally confessed he was interested.

For one year they had a crazy romance, which ended when she went away for vacation to visit her family. Just like that, Jay, who bores easily, moved on. And when she returned he was with Sky and she never forgave herself for losing her one true love. And now that she had a chance to be back with him that's exactly what she intended on doing.

"I really miss the older days," Melissa said as she touched Jay's hand. He still hadn't regained consciousness since his coma.

"I'm gonna let Jay know how much you've been here for him."

"You think he'll care?" Melissa asked walking up to her. "I mean, do you think he'll really consider being with me? I heard he was in love and —"

"Why wouldn't he?" She paused. "Parade hasn't been here since he was sent. She doesn't care about her husband. Or what happens to him."

"Whatever is happening between us is our business," Parade said entering the room. Melissa stood up and turned around to face Parade who was glaring at both women. "Who the fuck is this bitch, Melissa? And what is she doing around my husband?"

"I'm a friend," Quinn said.

"Well my husband can't consent to new friends in this state," Parade moved closer to her. "And since I'm his wife, I don't want no side bitches keeping time with what's mine." She paused. "Now get the fuck out."

Quinn swallowed the lump in her throat. In her mind she had plans to fight Parade tooth and nail if she ever laid eyes on her but now something about Parade's coldness caused her to shiver. And had she jumped, she would've gotten a taste of Parade's wreck game from back in the day.

"I'll talk to you later, Melissa," Quinn said touching her hand before leaving.

"Get the fuck out, Melissa," Parade said. "I wanna be alone with my husband."

"So now you wanna show up and boss me around?"

"Please," Parade said between heavy breaths. "Don't make me say it again 'cause it won't come out right."

Melissa looked at her and then Jay. "It don't make no difference. He ain't get up for his mama, he definitely not gonna get up for you. So I won't miss a thing." She snatched her purse and stormed out.

When they were alone Parade closed the door and walked up to the bed. Placing a hand on his head she took a deep breath. "Jay, it was hard for me to come here. It was hard because I, I know this my fault. And I want you to know that I'm gonna make things right." Tears rolled down her face and she took three quick breaths.

"Now I need you to do two things for me," she continued. "One is wake up because I...because I can't raise our family on my own right now. I'm not ready, Jay. And I'm trying to be ready but I'm not. So if you can hear my voice, if you can feel me its time to wake up, King. Please." She took another deep breath. "And when you're up I need you to forgive me for what I've done. You made some mistakes that caused us to lose our home and now I'm making more to put it back together again." She leaned down and kissed him. "I love you."

She walked toward the door, looked back once and walked out before calling Am'rak.

CHAPTER EIGHTEEN
PARADE

I walked into the motel room and tossed shopping bags on the bed. I had everything inside of them to secure the bag from Am'rak. There was no more beating around the bush with me. I had to go hard. I had to ask for what I wanted because time was running out. I needed to—

KNOCK. KNOCK. KNOCK.

Slowly I walked to the door and looked out the peephole. The person on the other side I loved but didn't want to see at the moment. But he deserved more respect from me so I put my big girl panties on and opened the door.

"Wayne..." I said walking toward the bed with him following me. I pushed the bags aside and flopped down on the edge of the mattress.

"Found a card with a credit balance huh?"

I nodded yes. "It was in my business name."

He sighed. "Where you going?"

"You already know."

"But didn't you say the man was strange and possibly a killer? And didn't you tell me that the night before he brought you back there was a dead man on the floor and—"

"Wayne, please." I said softly. "I still gotta do this. I told you that already and there ain't no talking me out of it."

He took a deep breath. "I know." He paused and dug into his purse, handing me a small gun. "Take this."

"Wayne, I don't—"

"Don't tell me you don't know how to shoot. 'Cause we both know you do. Just take it and use it if you need to."

I nodded. "Thank you." I tucked it in my purse.

"So have you talked to him?"

"He been calling ever since he dropped me off yesterday. Said for some reason he couldn't stop thinking about me."

"If you go you have to ask for the money, Parade. No beating around the bush."

"I'm not playing no games this time." I dug into my purse. "I wanted to show you something he gave me too. Not sure what it means but..." I handed him the card.

"What is this?"

"I don't know. But he acted as if it was the most important thing he could give me."

Wayne removed his phone from his pocket and took a picture. Then he handed the card back. "Don't know what it is but I'm gonna find out." He stood up. "Now, you do know if you ask for the whole stack you have to go the entire way. As far as sucking and fucking this trick goes."

"I know."

"Well, let's get it over with. Tell me what you gonna do."

Quinn sat in her truck in the parking lot of the motel she saw Parade enter earlier. She had the cell phone pressed against her ear and she was telling it all.

"Here she come right now," she said to Melissa on the phone. "What you want me to do?"

"Keep eyes on her."

"You mean follow her?"

"What you think?"

Quinn moved uneasily in her seat. "What if, I mean, what if she sees me?"

Silence.

Quinn looked at the screen and placed it back against her ear. "Mrs. Hernandez? Are you there?"

"I thought you wanted back in with my son," Melissa said firmly.

"I do but — "

"This is how it begins. If you can't do this you can't do nothing for me or Jay. Now follow that bitch and report back to me ASAP. I'm going to the hospital to see about my child."

When Quinn ended the call there was a knock at her window. She jumped when she saw Mercer standing there, holding a gun, the barrel in her direction. "Roll the window down," he said calmly.

She shook her head slowly from left to right, as tears welled up in her eyes.

"Don't make me hurt you." He paused. "I don't want to." Mercer had been sitting on the motel for Am'rak even though Parade didn't know she was being watched.

She believed him so she complied. "H…hello."

"Did you follow me?" Mercer asked.

Quinn moved uneasily in her seat and then she remembered who he was. "The hospital right?" She posed it more like a question instead of a fact.

"Yeah."

She nodded and placed both hands over her chest. "Good." She wiped fake sweat from her brow. "I thought you were crazy."

"What do you want?" He asked.

"You," she lied. "I followed your car when I saw you on the street."

He lowered the gun. "Why?"

"I wanted us to meet. Formally. I hope I didn't make you angry."

Quinn lay on the bed as Mercer stood over top of her jerking off. Naked from the waist up she thought him very odd but was more concerned about getting hurt, since she was certain he was affiliated with Parade in some strange way.

She was right.

With him being the friend of the stranger who kept time with Parade she had to be careful. More than it all she had to play smart.

After moaning loudly Mercer ejaculated on her belly. "I'm sorry," he said. "Want me to...eat you out or — "

"It's okay. I'm fine."

He got off the bed and extended his hand to help her to the bathroom. Running the water he smiled as he observed her. She was pretty. The kind of woman he could introduce to his mother if he had one. Sadly enough he never knew his family and but for Am'rak would be alone. And still, he would have to kill her knowing that Am'rak would never let him have her.

As she stood in front of him while he ran the water, which she would inevitably die in he said, "You're perfect."

She smiled; sensing something final was coming her way she started to think on her feet. "Thank you."

He nodded. "You like your water hot or — "

"I think I could fall in love with you." She paused. "You think you could ever, ever, learn to, to love me?"

His eyes widened. "How, why do you feel that way — "

"I don't know." She touched his face with her warm palm. "I just wanna take care of you." She was on her best performance ever. "Can I do that?"

In that moment, she had saved her own life.

AM'RAK

Am'rak pulled up in front of a chic restaurant in Washington DC. When a valet offered to take his car he extended a finger to halt him, in an effort to finish his call. "Aunt Quila, things are gonna work out," he said. "But you gonna have to trust me and try to calm down."

"But how can you be sure?"

"Because I have an idea that I'm putting into works right now." He paused. "Things will go as planned."

After his call ended he exited his ride and handed the valet attendant the keys to his Benz. He was about to walk inside when he squinted and saw her sitting in a black Honda Civic rental.

Fearing a set up because she was there early, he looked around from where he stood. When he couldn't call a foul, he bopped up to her car and knocked on the passenger side window. From where he was he could see that Parade was inside crying.

With Am'rak in view Parade wiped the tears from her face and unlocked the door. Concerned, Am'rak slipped inside and locked it behind himself. Examining her for a moment he asked, "What's wrong?"

She shrugged.

"If you didn't want to meet me it's – "

"It's not you." She wiped more tears away as she laid down initial steps to get the cash. "I mean, I wanted to be here it's just that, so much is going on in my private life and…and I don't know what to do."

He sat back in his seat and looked ahead. "Parade, you not out here alone. If something's on your mind, talk to me." He looked at her seriously. "We ain't been through a lot but we been through enough. What's up?"

She looked at him and took a deep breath. "The only thing on my mind right now is getting a drink and grabbing a meal. Can we do that?"

He placed his hand on her thigh and eased out the car. She followed him.

AM'RAK

Inside a luxury suite in Washington D.C., Am'rak just gave a room attendant a stack for the bottles of liquor on ice

BLACK AND THE UGLIEST

he ordered. He wasn't exactly sure why he agreed to go to the hotel as opposed to going to his Maryland crib, except when he asked Parade to go back to his house she seemed apprehensive and he understood why. First it was his ex blowing up his spot when she showed up uninvited, and next it was the intruders. So he figured going there would offer her a little comfort. And that finally she would spread them legs.

When he pushed the door open in the bedroom of the suite he was surprised to see Parade under the sheets apparently asleep.

Fuck. He said to himself. He had all intentions on finally feeling inside of her but now it looked like once again he was going to be short.

Placing the bucket on the table by the bed he slipped out of his navy blue POLO pants and eased under the covers with her. He almost choked on air when he realized she was completely naked and warm.

Slowly he guided his body so that he was directly behind her, the front of his boxers against her thick ass. Wrapping an arm around her waist he inhaled the coconut scent of her skin and moaned. His dick pulsated. To say she was sexy was an understatement that didn't need to be said. Everyone who laid eyes on her knew the truth.

Normally Am'rak would have already been stuffing her down by now but in his opinion Parade was fragile and there was a bigger picture in his mind. One that had nothing to do with sex. Say or do the wrong thing and she would probably be gone and her elusiveness was the reason he found her so interesting but also up for the unknown task ahead of her.

When she moaned a little and her fleshy ass cheeks backed into him his eyes widened. Maybe she wasn't asleep after all and that was all the invitation he needed. Slowly he ran his hand up and down her warm thighs as he kissed her back softly. She moaned slightly and moved a little more but in his opinion she was going to fake to the highest degree so he was going to allow her the honor. It didn't mean he wasn't going to dig into the pussy though.

When she backed into him again, he positioned her on her back, crawled on top of her and smiled. Her eyes were open as she stared at him seductively. "I'm afraid of you," she said.

"Don't be."

He reached to his left, got a condom and eased it on his thick dick. "I just wanna..." Before he finished his sentence he was inside of her, deeply. Pushing. Stirring. Pulsing.

"Damn, you feel so..." She pulled him toward her so that his chest pressed against her warm breasts. Placing her lips against his ear she said, "What took you so long?"

He chuckled once. "You were playing games."

She kissed the side of his face and then his lips. "Nah. Just prefer to do things on my time that's all." She eased on top of him and looked down at his face. And then, as if he belonged to her, she surfed back and forth on top of him.

He licked his lips as he stiffened inside of her even more. This was not a side he saw in the past and yet he loved her strength and power. And more than anything in the moment her fuck game which was official.

Placing his hands on the sides of her waist he pumped into her harder and longer until her head fell back and her mouth opened.

"Fuck, Parade...you feel so good."

She looked down at him. "You feel better."

They pumped and touched each other until they were out of breath and drifted into a deep sleep. Moments later, while her eyes were closed, he rolled over and looked at her. He figured she was playing games again so he spoke his peace.

"I need you to do something for me," he said. "Something that will help me a lot. You do that, and I'll give you anything you desire. That much I promise."

PARADE

I was driving my rental after leaving Am'rak when Wayne called. I almost didn't answer because I knew he would bash me for not taking things further and asking for the cash but I had a plan.

"Parade, why didn't you ask for the money?" He snapped. "Fuck is wrong with you?"

"I'm gonna ask, Wayne." I stopped at the light. "It's just that it seemed too hot to—"

"After you gave him the pussy?" Wayne continued. "Parade, I'm not feeling this situation at all."

"I'm gonna do it. Especially since he asked me for a favor."

"A favor? You fucked the nigga! That should be enough."

"Maybe it's not," I said. "I mean, if I do whatever he wants maybe I can earn the money another way."

"Well I got some friends of mine looking into him and—"

"Wayne, why you doing that?" I yelled.

"Doing what? Making sure my best friend lives long enough to live out her dreams of being reunited with her family?"

"No, get in my business and tell the world I'm fucking over my husband."

"Parade, I just want to—"

"I gotta go." I hung up and pulled in front of the hospital.

Taking a deep breath, I wiped the tears that started to creep in my eyes. I mean, what was he thinking doing something so stupid without asking? It was bad enough I had to put myself out there to find Am'rak but now he was making things worse. And there was no way I was letting Am'rak get away without asking for the money but I had to be smart. And since I knew he really liked me, even called me two times while on my way to the hospital, I felt confident that things would be fine and within time the money would be mine.

Walking into the hospital I signed in and caught the elevator up to Jay's room. When I made it to the hallway I saw a group of familiar male faces taking the steps in the opposite direction. It looked like they came out of Jays' room but I wasn't sure.

When I made it to his door I saw Melissa talking to the bed and when I walked further inside I saw Jay. Quinn was there too and I was five seconds from snatching her by the hair until I saw what was happening. He was up!

I immediately felt weak at the knees when I gazed on his opened eyes. And when he saw me and smiled my heart melted.

"Bae," he said reaching out for me. "I fucking missed you."

I dropped my purse at the door and rushed over to him. First I kissed his face and then I kissed his lips and then his face and lips again. All the while, Melissa stood around watching. What the fuck was up with this chick?

"I can't believe you're up!" I kissed him again. "I can't believe…"

"Of course you can't believe it," Melissa interrupted, walking closer to the bed. "You haven't been here much."

"Ma," Jay said. "What I tell you about starting shit. Let it go. Besides," he looked at me. "I'm sure she had a reason."

"I hear all that but son, there's a lot you don't know that you need to about her."

"And what's that?"

"What is wrong with you?" I snapped. "Your son just woke up from a coma and you use the moment to shit on our marriage? Then you add insult to injury by having this bitch back in here when I told you both I never wanted to see her again!"

Silence.

"Ma, she's right," Jay said softly. "Things ain't been square and I'm to blame for that. And I appreciate you being here but now," he took a deep breath. "Look, give me some alone time with my wife."

"But, Jay —"

"Please, ma!" He snapped. "I'll talk to you in a minute."

"And take this whore with you!" I said referring to Quinn.

Melissa looked at me and then Jay before walking out with that bitch.

When they were gone I smiled. "How do you feel?"

"Bae, all I can say is that I'm happy to be alive and even more happy to see your face." He paused. "I mean, I know I was in a coma but at the same time I could feel myself wanting to get back to you."

I stared at him for the next few minutes, just squeezing and rubbing his hand. "I, prayed for you to come back to me. And the next day you do just that. I love you so much, Jay."

"Bae, there's something I want to—"

"Listen, I'm going to get the house back," I told him cutting him off. I had a feeling he was going to bring up losing our home so I wanted to ease his mind. The last thing I needed was him having another heart attack.

His eyebrows rose. "H...how?"

"Don't worry about how. I just..." I squeezed his hand tighter. "I love you so much, Jay and I want you to forgive me. Forgive me for driving you to get into the accident."

"Parade—"

"And forgive me for being so hard on you while—"

"Parade, you have to hear me out!"

"Jay, just forgive me for what I had to do." I leaned in and kissed his forehead. "I'll be back soon to take you home. I promise you that." I walked out.

MERCER

Mercer sat in his car across the parking lot from Parade's rental at the hospital. He was talking to Am'rak. When she walked out he picked up his phone. "She's back out. Want me to follow her?"

"Yeah, but after that go back to the hospital," Am'rak said. "Get as much information as you can on what she was doing there. I need leverage in case she doesn't bite on my future plan."

"Already on it."

CHAPTER NINETEEN
JAY

My mother, I love her but she's too much at times. Always wanting me to be her kid son and never understanding that I was a man, with a wife and kids of my own. Things were different from when I was ten.

I had just finished eating a cheese sandwich when my mother and Quinn walked inside the room. I sat up straight, wiped my mouth and looked at my mother. "What's Quinn doing back here?" I asked. "You heard Parade. She shouldn't be here."

"Don't get mad, Jay," my mother said. "We were having such a nice conversation before Parade showed up and ruined it all."

"I asked you a question," I said firmer. "What is she doing back here?"

"Jay," Quinn said walking up to the right side of the bed. In the same place my wife stood yesterday. "I, I know you don't want to see me now but there's so much I have to tell you. So much I think you should know."

"Listen, if my wife comes back and see's you in my room the first step I take will be to get outta this bed and kill you."

"JAY HERNANDEZ!" My mother yelled. "This woman has been at your side since you been in a coma! The least you could do is offer her a little respect by hearing her out."

I took a deep breath. I didn't understand what was happening. I didn't understand why my mother was pushing shit so hard with this chick. I just woke up and already my moms was thrusting another bitch on me when she knew how I felt about my wife.

Taking another deep breath I said, "What you wanna say, Quinn?"

"Like your mother said," she cleared her throat. "I, um, have been here since —"

"You gonna tell me or not?" I snapped looking at the door again hoping Parade wouldn't come back. This accident although fucked up may have saved my marriage. I didn't need Quinn messing that up.

"Your wife, I think she's cheating on you," she said. "And I know you don't want to hear that but it's the truth."

I frowned. "Fuck you mean cheating on me?" I positioned myself so I could see her clearly. And I can't lie; my heart was pumping just thinking about what she was going to say next.

"I followed her because, well, she was acting strange and I—"

"Get out." I waved the air. "Get the fuck out of my room."

"Jay, please." My mother said. "Just listen."

"GET OUT!" I yelled. "NOW!" Quinn looked at my mother and ran out the room crying. When she was gone I looked at my mom. "You too."

"Son, please don't."

"Ma, don't make me say it again." I said.

She grabbed her purse. "I'll bring the kids by tomorrow."

I nodded and she walked out.

When I was alone I rubbed my throbbing temples. I don't know what they were talking about, or what they meant by trying to fuck my head up when it came to my wife but I didn't play games when it came to my family. Parade may have been mad at me for losing our home but she would never cheat on me.

I had to get out of this bed.

Now!

PARADE

I had just finished making breakfast for my kids when I turned around and noticed Logan wasn't at the table again. I sat down the long plates of eggs, bacon and potatoes.

"Want me to get him, ma?" Landon asked.

I smiled. "No, I'll go."

I scooped Logan up some food, walked to the room he slept in and knocked on the door. "Come in." He said with an attitude.

I walked inside. "Hungry?"

He nodded yes and took the plate. Immediately he started eating.

"Logan, how much longer are you gonna hate me?"

"I don't hate you."

"Then what is it?"

"I hate that you, I mean, I hate that ya'll just moved us from our life and put us here. And…you know what, it doesn't matter."

I sat next to him. "I'm sorry we didn't ask you your input." I said placing my hand on his knee. "Things

T. STYLES   167

moved so quickly that we didn't get a chance to ask you kids what you wanted. But I promise you this, that will never, ever, happen again. I—" When my phone rang I looked down at it and pulled it out my pocket. "I have to answer—"

"It's okay, ma," he smiled. "I don't feel like fighting anymore. I understand."

"Really?"

He nodded.

I kissed his cheek, walked out the room and into my own. Sitting down on the edge of the bed I answered. "Hello."

"Somebody forgot 'bout me already."

"Never." I said when I heard Am'rak's voice. Today was the day I was going to hit him for the money so I had to be sweet. "What you doing right now?"

"Waiting on you."

I nodded. "Okay, give me a few hours. I'll be on the way."

"I'm here."

"Ma," Ella said knocking on the door.

I placed my hand over the phone and said, "I'll be right out." When she was gone I put the phone back to my ear. "Hello."

"Everything cool?" Am'rak asked.

Good. He didn't hear my daughter. The last thing I wanted was a dangerous man knowing about my family. He already knew my real name, which was way too much. "Yes, of course." I cleared my throat. "I'll see you in a little while."

When I hung up I walked out to see Wayne in the kitchen smiling at me. I could tell before he even opened his mouth that something was wrong and I didn't know if I could handle it at the moment. "Are you okay?" I asked him. "Are Danny and Shantay alright?"

"Come...Let's talk outside."

"You scaring me."

"Please." He smiled and grabbed my hand.

We walked outside and I closed the door. "What's going on, Wayne?"

He took a deep breath. "I'm going back to L.A."

My mouth opened and closed. "But...I..."

"I'm sorry. I really wanted to stay but my husband threatened to leave and you know...I can't have that." He paused. "Danny is my foundation and I may be a tough girl but that's one thing I can't deal with."

I moved closer and grabbed both of his hands. "Wayne, please stay for just a few more days. I'm finally about to ask for the money and —"

"I can't do that, Parade. I mean didn't you hear me?" He said softly. "My husband is gonna leave me, baby. Now I love you. I'm sure you know I would die for you too but I can't…I just can't let him leave me."

I took a deep breath. Despite the blessings I had received with my husband being alive, the selfishness in me wasn't trying to let my best friend go until I brought my entire family back home. We came together and I wanted us to leave together.

"Okay. Wait here." I went in the house and grabbed the gun he loaned me and gave it back to him. "Bye."

He smiled, walked up close and kissed me on the cheek. "I love you."

I nodded, too selfish to let him hear the words back. He stood and waited but what he wanted me to say wouldn't leave my lips. So he got into his car and pulled off.

PARADE

When I made it to Am'rak's house and knocked on the door he yelled, "Come in, bae."

I entered and was surprised to see him sitting on the couch in the living room, a suitcase on top of the table. I smiled at him. "What's going on?"

"Come here."

I nodded and walked closer. "Is everything okay?"

"I heard you in a bind." He sat back. "Is that true?"

I swallowed the lump in my throat and suddenly the floor seemed hot. I paced a little, trying to find the right thing to say. "I...I'm confused on what you talking about."

He nodded and stood up. "Sit down, Parade."

"Am'rak, I—"

"Sit the fuck down!"

The thunder of his voice ripped through my chest and I flopped down on the sofa.

"Open the suitcase," he said softer.

I did what he asked. When the latch was open I saw stacks of one hundred dollar bills inside. "What is this?"

"One hundred grand."

My eyes widened. "But, I don't understand."

"Yes you do." He paused. "You were gonna ask me for the money right? That's what this all been about? The holding out on sex. The elusiveness when I asked you about your life. You wanted the money...so there it is."

I felt as if my life was about to be over forever. And suddenly, that quickly, I didn't want the money anymore. I don't know where I was going to go or where my family and me were going to live but in that moment, none of it mattered. I just wanted to leave and hug them all again. More than anything I wanted us all to be safe.

I stood up. "Am'rak, maybe—"

I don't know when it happened but when I opened my eyes I was looking at his black Balenciaga boots from the floor. The taste of blood in my mouth.

"Yeah, all of this was a game," he yelled over me. "All of this was a ploy to get at my money!" He continued. "And chump change at that. If you would've asked I would've given you the paper. All you had to do was be honest. But nah, you wanna play games, toss a nigga some pussy and then run off with his racks." Slowly he stooped down and rubbed my face with the back of his hand.

"Am'rak, can you tell me what you mean?"

"I got Intel on you, Parade. Some faggies been asking around about me and my man got his hand on one of 'em." He paused. "Turns out you married to some Spanish nigga who fucked up the paper back in L.A. and now you back here slumming."

Wayne, no! I knew this would happen! I thought to myself. I begged him not to have his friends asking around about him and now my worst fears came to be realized.

"I know you got three kids. I know his name is Jay Hernandez and that you Mrs. Parade Hernandez."

I felt faint.

"And guess what, I'm gonna give you the money," he continued. "But it's gonna cost you."

JAY

"You did a good job but you should take it easy for the rest of the day," my nurse said as she helped me back to bed. I had been practicing walking and I think she thought it was too much on me. Maybe it was. "You had a long day, especially with your kids visiting earlier."

"Maybe you're right," I said thinking about their faces. They looked healthy but sad and it motivated me even more to move. "I guess they inspired me to do what I gotta do to get back."

"Yes but you must take it easy." She said with a smile. "We want you at your very, very best."

I nodded. "Thank you."

When she left I lay back in bed and took a deep breath. Suddenly a man sitting in a wheelchair rolled into my room. He was wearing a black backpack and his eyes were sinister. Without saying a word he reminded me of the worst niggas I knew on the street. "So you up."

I frowned. "Who you?"

"I'm nobody really," he smiled. "I was shot around the time they brought you in. Glad to see we both came through 'bout the same time. It looked bad at first."

I didn't trust this dude but I didn't know why either. Not only that but I was vulnerable. If he wanted to act a fool there would be nothing I could do but watch. Immediately my mind went to the people I wronged in life. And outside of the banks I was coming up short.

"Who are you?" I repeated.

He smiled and slowly got up. Closing the door he walked up to me. I sat on the edge of the bed. Not sure what I was gonna be able to do because every part of my body ached. But I knew one thing, I was going out swinging.

"I always wanted to be an actor so, well, forgive me if I came at you the wrong way."

"Fuck you want with me, nigga?"

"Okay, I can tell you want me to get to the point." He reached behind him for his backpack and tossed it on the bed next to me. I scooted away from it and glared.

"Fuck kind of games is this?"

"That's from Parade. While you were in your coma she had a whole new life with my man. And she asked me to give you that money for whatever bill you got. Then she wanted me to tell you to head back to L.A. 'cause ain't nothing left here for you."

My temples throbbed and my heart rocked out my chest. And still I was on my feet, with no cane. Slowly I moved toward him. "If you knew me, you'd know better than to play games when it came to my wife."

"The money's all there," he said slyly. "So don't shoot the messenger. Especially not one who just saved your life. Your wife had a wish and she used it on you. Be grateful. Most bitches out here foul."

"Who are you?"

"Mercer." He winked and walked out the door.

I watched him leave before flopping on the edge of the bed. When I opened the bag I saw racks inside. There was also a card that read *Te concedo un deseo*, which meant *I grant you one wish* in Spanish.

What was going on? I know Parade wouldn't, she wouldn't do this to me.

I...I'm not understanding nothing right now.

I picked up my phone and called my moms. "Hey, I need you to come back to the hospital."

"Is everything okay?"

"Nah, you gotta come get me, now."

CHAPTER TWENTY
DAYS LATER
JAY

When I made it to my mother's house my boys helped me through the door. I was always the strong one in the family and now I was relying on them. It had been a long time coming and finally I was almost on my feet, able to walk without assistance. Even though I was alive, I felt dead because I don't know what was going on with my wife. But I did know this, I had no intention on leaving Maryland until I found out where she was and why she left.

After I sat down on the sofa I told my children to go to the room so I could talk to my mother who was making Spanish rice in the kitchen. In the past I loved when she cooked that meal but I wasn't in the mood to eat.

"Ma, come here right quick!"

"Give me a second," she said cheerfully. "I'm making dinner and—"

"Ma!" I yelled. "Ven aqui, now!"

A minute later she came out wiping her hand on a yellow towel. Slowly she sat next to me. "What's wrong, Jay? You feel alright?"

"I need you to," I cleared my throat because I had been trying to act like Parade was visiting friends. Didn't want her to know what was really going on because I knew she would judge her. Now it was time to ask questions. "I need you to tell me everything you know about Parade."

She rolled her eyes. "Jay, why is everything that exits your mouth about that woman?"

I stared at her.

She sighed and rubbed her hands down her thighs. "All I know is that while you were in the hospital she was spending less time with her kids, less time seeing you and less time asking how she could help raise her family. Is that a woman you want at your side?"

I frowned and ran my hand down my face. "Where she go?" She looked away and I knew she knew more than she was letting on. "Mami, I love you. I do. But understand this, if you're holding out on info I need to find my wife I'll never fuck with you again."

"Find her? I didn't know she was missing." She said.

I clinched my jaw. "Just tell me what I asked, please."

She took a deep breath. "If you want real answers you need to call Quinn. She knows more than I do."

JAY

Two days later, using a cane, I was walking out of my mother's house to Quinn's truck. She promised to help find my wife and I hoped she would do that without trying anything else. "Hey," I said when I slid into the passenger seat. "Thanks for this."

"You need any help?"

"I'm fine." I said louder than I wanted. "I mean, thank you but I'm good."

She smiled. "I'm glad I can do this for you."

I wiped my hand down my face. "Listen, Quinn, I'm sorry that my mother pulled you into this. I don't know what her purpose was and I don't know what she thought would happen between us but my position is firm when it comes to my family. And I gotta let you know that I'm not leaving Parade. Ever."

She looked down at the steering wheel.

"Please don't get me wrong," I continued. "I'm grateful for anything you may have done to help out at the hospital but—"

"When you were in my palm you responded to me. Got hard. Could you feel my touch?"

I frowned. "What you talking about?"

She looked at me.

I repositioned myself in the seat. "Are you saying you...gripped me...on my...when...when I was out?"

"Yes."

My jaw hung and then I took a deep breath. Quinn was always weird which was another reason I dumped her for Sky back in the day. And I can see after all this time nothing had changed.

"If that's how you get off then—"

"How could you even marry her?" She snapped. "I remember you in school, Jay. And she wasn't your type. At least with Sky it made sense but now..."

"She's more my type than you know." I smirked.

"But why?" She yelled. "You always told me I would be next if—"

"Why you bringing up shit I said when I was a kid?" I snapped. "I'm a grown man now, Quinn. With a family and that's all I'm thinking about. Don't let the cane fool you. I know what I'm saying." I paused. "Can you understand that?"

Silence.

"Quinn, can you understand?"

She looked at me, turned the truck on and pulled off. I just hoped I had my answer.

Thirty minutes later we were outside a house that she said the nigga who works for the guy who got Parade brought her to. Said he told her it was his boss's spot.

I made a call and twenty minutes later my friend showed up in a black pickup. Once there, they pulled up behind Quinn's truck and walked over to us.

"Which one?"

"That one," I said pointing. I positioned myself to get out but my man Erick stopped me by shoving the truck door lightly.

"You called us." He said. "Let us do our thing."

I nodded and five minutes later him and two other dudes I didn't know were banging on the door. I hated that my body wasn't one hundred percent and I had to sit and watch other niggas handle business for me but for now I needed to let somebody else help. After two minutes of banging there was no sign of anybody being home and then Erick kicked in the door.

"Uh, maybe you should go," I told Quinn when he kicked things up to the next level. "I'll hang out with them. Don't wanna get you in the mix."

"I'm not leaving without you."

I looked at her and shook my head. If she wanted to hang back that was on her. Within seconds Erick and his boys were running through the house while I sat anxiously in the car waiting on the verdict.

Five minutes later Erick returned alone with my wife nowhere in sight. "She not in there, man." He said. "You want us to call around and—"

"Nah, I'm good." My jaw twitched.

"You sure?"

I nodded.

"Well I'm here if you need me. Just say the word." He looked at the house. "You may wanna roll out though. Don't know if the neighbors called the police. But hit me if you need me." I shook his hand; he hit the truck once and walked to the pickup truck.

With no other moves in play, Quinn pulled off while I sat back frustrated in the passenger seat. I couldn't believe this was happening. I mean, did Parade really choose another nigga all because of the mistake I made?

"I have a number," Quinn said softly.

BLACK AND THE UGLIEST

"What number?" I sighed, looking at the road.

"Of the guy she left with."

I looked at her. "Pull over up there." We were about five blocks away from the house so I figured that was good enough. "Why you just telling me this now?"

"You didn't ask." She paused. "Just told me to take you to the house and that's what I did."

I frowned. "How you get the number?"

"Well...remember when you were in the hospital and I was trying to tell you how I followed Parade?"

I rolled my eyes, "Yeah."

"So, I followed her to a motel and saw the guy who lives in that house. He was with her and Mercer. Mercer is the dude I said that likes me. A little too much. Anyway, we met each other and let's just say we connected and he gave me his number."

"Connected huh?"

"Yeah."

I frowned because I recognized the name Mercer from the hospital. "Call him."

She removed her cell phone from her pocket and dialed a number before placing it on speaker. "Mercer, this is..."

"I know who you are," he said. "Is he with you?"

She frowned. "Wait, you know I know Jay?"

"I know you just showed up to the house with him. And that Am's neighbors saw niggas going through his crib." He paused. "Now where is he?"

"I'm right here." I said. "And she ain't know nothing 'bout that. It's all on me. Now where's my wife?"

"Hold on."

The anticipation felt like forever and finally after two minutes Parade came to the phone and said, "Hello."

I exhaled and moved uneasily in the seat. Just hearing her voice after days of not being able to put me at ease before I even knew what she was about to say. "Parade, what's going on? Why you moving with niggas out here when you know how I am? I'm about to kill everybody!"

"What you want, Jay?"

I frowned. "I wanna know why you got some nigga bringing me money and—"

"Jay, take the money and save the house."

"I don't want the fucking house!" I yelled punching the air, missing Quinn's face by inches. "I want you."

"Well we over!" She yelled. "You really think I would be with you after everything you did? After you had our children put out of our home?" She paused.

"I'm not interested in being married to a man like you," she said in a low voice. "It's...it's over."

"Parade, don't do this!"

"Don't call me again, Jay."

"PARADE!"

Silence.

"PARADE!"

"You done," an unfamiliar voice asked on the phone.

"Who the fuck is this?"

"It don't matter," he said. "You got the money. I got the girl. Be gone."

"You better watch your back," I said.

"Forget about your wife. Or I'll help you do that by erasing you, your kids and the rest of your life off this planet."

PARADE

Now that Am'rak had me for what he wanted, he moved us back down south and I was more confused than ever. Why did he want me so badly? I had yet to get a complete answer. Something was missing.

I had just put the last of my new clothes in drawers in the bedroom, which were part of the expensive reinvention efforts when I broke down crying on the bed. I missed my kids. I missed my friends and I missed my husband. The way I talked to him on the phone was harsh but I needed him to move on. I had a feeling what Am'rak was capable of and that scared me.

Still, there was no way I could see spending a lifetime with Am'rak but what could I do? I wasn't even sure if he gave Jay the money like he claimed when I elected to use the card. I think he likes to play games.

I was still crying when the bedroom door flew open. He came inside drinking something brown in a small glass. He drank more and more which made me uncomfortable.

"You crying again?"

Silence.

"Answer me." He snapped, moving deeper into the room.

"Am'rak, what do you want with me?" I asked. "I don't get it. I mean, why you doing this?"

"Where's the latest dress I bought for you?"

"What dress?"

His brows lowered. "You playing games now?"

I looked away and remembered the box in the bottom of the closet. "I didn't open it yet. I'm sorry."

"Well open it and get dressed. We have a long day ahead of us." He walked out.

ONE WEEK LATER

JAY

I just finished moving the last box back into our house in L.A. when someone knocked on the door. I ordered pizza for the kids because I didn't feel like cooking so I figured it was them. To be honest I didn't feel like doing anything.

It felt better to be home but the constant questions from my friends about where Parade was weighed on me. I didn't feel like telling them that I fucked up my life and because of it my wife didn't want me back.

Still, that's exactly what happened.

"Logan, get the door!" I yelled after putting up the curtains in the living room. I was almost back to myself but still needed more help than I wanted these days. So small chores like furnishing the house was difficult.

I was almost done when I saw Wayne walk up to me. "What you want?"

"What I want?" He said wiping his long hair out of his right eye and toward his left. "Why didn't you tell me you were home?" He looked around from where he stood.

"You not my wife."

"Jay, where is my friend?"

I laughed.

"Jay!" He said walking closer. "I been calling for days and I couldn't reach Parade or you. Now what's going on?"

"Why you in here faking like you care?" I snapped. "If you really gave a fuck then you would've stayed instead of tucking tail and running back here to Hollywood."

He took a deep breath and for some reason I felt bad. Don't get me wrong, I'm not with the gay shit but Wayne had always come through when we needed him, especially when it came to the kids.

"I'm sorry about that," I said grabbing my cane that was leaning on the wall to take a seat on the sofa. "I'm just...I'm just trying to keep it together but it's hard, Wayne. I can't even pump fake."

"Don't worry about it." He sat next to me.

"Nah, you didn't deserve that shit." I wiped my hand down my face. "It's just that, I think I messed up big time, Wayne. And I'm pretty sure Parade ain't ever coming back."

"How you figure?"

"She left me."

He laughed.

"I pour out my heart and you laugh in my face?"

"Listen, I've known Parade all my life. And leaving you ain't in her makeup. Trust me."

"And I have known her almost just as long, Wayne. Trust *me* when I say she's gone."

"Not saying you don't know her." He paused. "But what I'm telling you is what I know about my friend. That woman loves you. To the impossible limits of this universe. And there ain't no way she would leave you in her own will. None."

"Well why am I back in L.A. without her?"

"That's what I'm gonna have to find out."

"You can try all you want," I paused. "But I heard it with my own ears. She's done with me. Left me for some nigga that dropped the paper to get the house back—"

"Jay, no!" Wayne said covering his mouth.

"What?"

"Jay, please don't tell me he has her!" He was trembling.

I stood up. "What you mean?"

"I have to go." He ran toward the door.

"Go where?"

"Back to Maryland to find my friend!" He rushed out the door.

CHAPTER TWENTY-ONE
WAYNE

I was packing a black duffle bag heading back to Maryland when Adrian walked in our bedroom door, eyes all wide and crazy. "Not now, Aid. Please save the speeches for the pageant."

"Not now?" He yelled. "Bitch, what you talking 'bout?" He stood next to me. "And more importantly where you going?"

"You already know."

He flopped on the edge of my bed. "Miss Wayne, if you go you gonna lose your husband. If you go you gonna lose your family." He paused. "And you know I love Shantay but she's as foul as the inside of a restaurant dumpster when you not home. Don't leave us with that child alone!"

I rolled my eyes.

"I'm serious, Wayne!" He continued. "We do our best but she got way too many gay fabulous mothers to take us seriously anymore."

I sat next to him. "My Parade is in trouble."

"Your Parade is always in fucking trouble."

"But this is different," I paused. "I'm afraid," I took a deep breath. "I'm afraid if I don't go back that she'll die. Think about it, Aid. When was the last time you heard me speak in such ways?"

He looked down. "Can't lie, it's been awhile." He sighed. "But still, I don't understand why you never think of us as much as you do her."

"Blasphemy."

"No it's not." He paused. "Anytime Parade is in trouble you drop everything, even your family and run. I've seen you walk away from lucrative business deals at our restaurant to defend her honor too. And it's been that way for as long as I can remember."

"How do you feel about yourself?" I asked him.

"Bitch, I'm everything. The mecca! The queen! The last. The first. The ending. The beginning." He stood up and started fluffing his hair. "The beautiful, the fabulous—"

"You see?" I said softly. "You don't look like a person who needs anything but love. Parade does."

He flopped next to me. "Ooohhh…that's sneaky. Gonna ask a queen how she feels about herself just to prove a point." He pointed at me. "Real low."

I shrugged. "Parade has always needed me. And I thought when we moved here that she realized how much she's worth and how much she's loved but I fear being in a city where beauty and wealth is more important may have made her worse." Tears rolled down my cheek. "And I have to find her, Aid. Can you understand that?"

He nodded.

I stood up and grabbed my duffle bag while walking to the door. I was almost out when he ran and hugged me tightly from behind. I smiled and walked out.

When I went downstairs I was surprised to see Danny standing in the middle of the living room with his arms folded over his chest. "This how you do me?"

"Baby, I was going to call you." I stood in front of him and dropped my bag on the floor.

"You were gonna call me and then leave?" He paused. "Like I'm some trick?"

"Danny."

"FUCK THAT!" He yelled. "How come you the only one who gets to make moves without dealing with the consequences, Wayne?" He moved closer. "Huh? What have I done in our relationship to be treated so badly?"

"I'm going to help Parade."

"You always going to fucking help Parade. Who's gonna help this marriage? Who's gonna help this family?"

"Daddy," Shantay said walking down the steps. "Is everything okay?"

"Shantay, come with me," Adrian said walking down the steps and up to her. "I have some new dresses I want you to try on at my place."

Shantay smiled at him and they walked out the door. I took a deep breath. "Danny, please don't fight me on this. I'm begging you."

"And what exactly does your begging mean to me? I'm a man, Wayne. But I still need somebody to love me. So tell me how can begging help me with that?"

"I have to do this but I don't want to worry about not having a family waiting when I get back."

"By the sight of that duffle it looks like it's a chance you're willing to take." He said looking down at it.

"Danny."

"You know what, you gonna do what you want so go." He walked to the front door and opened it. "Leave."

"Danny!"

"If you gonna go get the fuck out!"

I looked at him as tears rolled down my face. There was no need in me fighting with him. When he was this mad it was best to separate and talk to him when things were calmer. So I grabbed my bag off the floor, walked out the door and when I turned around he was behind me.

I blinked a few times. "Where you going?" I asked.

"You don't think I'm letting you go on some wild goose chase alone do you?" He grabbed his keys from his pocket and unarmed the alarm on his car. Next he opened the passenger side door. "Now get in."

I smiled and ran up to him, before kissing him passionately. "I love you so much."

"I know you do." He paused. "That's the only reason I'm still here."

We almost made it to the street when Jay pulled in front of Danny's car, blocking our exit. Danny backed up and allowed him inside. He parked in our driveway, grabbed his bag and exited his truck. Hopping a little, he opened the backseat of Danny's car and slid inside.

"Good," Jay said. "I caught you just in time."

"How you know we were leaving for Maryland?" Danny asked.

Jay looked at me. "You really asking me that?"

Danny looked at me and they broke out laughing. I guess they had their answers.

DAYS LATER
MARYLAND
JAY

I had just finished taking a shower when the door opened and Quinn walked inside the bathroom with a folded towel in her hands. She smiled at me and I took it before wrapping it around my body. "I forgot to give you one," she said.

"So you waited to give it to me until I got out the shower?"

She grinned. "Jay, to be honest, I'm just happy that you're here. And that I have enough space in my house to help you and your friends. I won't push myself on you unless you want me to."

"I'm married."

"I know." She sighed. "Trust me I know." She took another deep breath. "Dinner's ready. Wayne and Danny are downstairs waiting on you."

She was about to walk out when I said, "Quinn."

She stopped at the door and turned around. "Yes."

"I just wanted to say...well I wanted to say thank you."

She smiled again and walked out.

Twenty minutes later I was downstairs sitting at the table with Wayne and his husband. I'ma be real, I fuck with Wayne but being apart of this situation was not something I saw myself getting used to. With homosexuals and all. Like even now they can't keep their hands off each other. Touching, hugging and kissing like I'm with this shit. I'm like hold off on that until you get in your own crib.

"Yah, mind?" I said to Wayne who was seated on my right and Danny who was seated on his left.

Quinn touched my leg and I held out my hand. I didn't need nobody trying to quiet me.

"What you mean, man?" Danny asked.

"I came all the way back to Maryland with you and him hugging and kissing like it was going out of style." I paused. "I thought this was about Parade. Can we take a break from this shit now?"

"It is about Parade," Wayne said.

"So can you cut it out for five minutes?"

Danny leaned back and folded his arms across his chest. "We're here because we care about Parade too."

"I'm not saying—"

"Don't cut me off, Jay," he said. "Hear me out." He paused. "Now we here because we care about your wife. And you may not agree with my lifestyle but Wayne is mine and I'm not gonna be ashamed of him. Wasted too much time doing that already and I'm not gonna spend another second doing it again." He continued. "So you want our help or not?"

I leaned up and clasped my hands together on the table. "What we gonna do?" My teeth gritted.

"Mercer," Quinn said.

I looked at her. "What about him?"

"He called again last night." She paused. "Gave me a new number. Said he had to trash the last phone. I think because his boss told him too."

"You think you could meet with him?" Wayne asked her. "Maybe somewhere private so we could talk to him?"

She shrugged. "I don't know about that. I mean, when you guys were in L.A. he stood me up a few different times when we had plans. Still mad about Jay breaking into that house I think. We were supposed to go to dinner and stuff but like I said...I mean...he doesn't seem interested now."

"He's interested," Danny said. "Just cautious."

"What's up with that dude?" I asked.

"I don't know but I think he be following me to work," Quinn continued.

I frowned. "He came to your house too?"

"No, I always go out the way to get here ever since I saw him out my window one day while working. It's like he wants to get to know me but he's afraid."

I looked at Danny for some reason. I guess because he use to be a cop and I was so desperate at this moment I needed some direction to be able to find Parade. At first I thought she left me on her own but after I saw Wayne's face when he came to my house I knew I got it wrong. Then I started putting one and one together and remembered her coming to the hospital and apologizing in advance. She even said she'd get us back into the house, which she did. It's like she knew she had to do something but I doubt she thought things would go this far.

Still, why would she think I would want her to use her body? Why would she think that I'd like my wife to sell herself for...I mean...just thinking about it got me wanting to spazz the fuck out.

"Okay, this may go a little differently than we thought." I said. "But I don't want you to reach out to him anymore. From here on out let him call you because I don't want him being suspicious."

"I can do that."

"But you can't fall in love with him," Danny said. "You can't like him or have anything to do with him seriously. This nigga may die and—"

"I could never fall for him," Quinn said looking at me. "I'm only in love with one person."

Wayne side eyed her. "What does that mean?"

Quinn looked at Wayne and then me. "I'll clean up." She got up and took my plate and hers off the table leaving Wayne and Danny's.

Wayne glared at me. "Can I talk to you?" He asked me. "In private?"

Five minutes later we were in the backyard. "I know you don't have us here with a girl who wants you?" Wayne asked.

"What you expect me to do?" I paused. "Not use her? As far as I'm concerned she's the only one who seeing a nigga associated with the dude who got my wife."

"That woman is in love with you."

"I get all that," I paused. "But I'm not interested." I sat down on a lawn chair. "Besides, my wife keep that body right."

He frowned and sat down. "What does that mean, Jay?"

"Parade always made me proud," I said honestly. "It's like, whenever we stepped out she looked the part."

He looked at me and then the lawn. "It all makes sense now."

I glared at him. "What does that mean?"

"I always wondered why my friend, after all this time, still felt the need to look or be something else. And now I see that it's you."

"Excuse me?"

"Do you know how she keeps it so tight with running a popular salon for hours a day? Do you know how she keeps it tight with caring for three kids and making sure they get to school, do their homework and cook dinner for you when you get home?"

I shrugged.

"Plastic surgery, Jay."

I frowned and leaned back. "You playing right?"

Silence.

I stood up, walked a few feet out and then turned to look at him. "Parade was going to a surgeon?"

"Yes and now I understand why. I only been out here with you for five minutes and already I got a complex."

"I never gave my wife a fucking complex!" I yelled pointing at him. "I let my wife know how sexy her body is everyday and—"

"What if she wasn't sexy?" He said standing up. "What if something happened to her face? Would you love her still?"

"Don't ask me no stupid shit like that."

"I'm asking!"

"Yes I would!"

"Well she didn't know that, Jay." He paused. "I'm her best friend and I'm telling you she didn't know. At the very least she didn't feel comfortable enough to believe it."

Hearing that I made my wife do anything to her body had me fucked up in the head. I was always against surgery so I'm not understanding why she would think I would think...I mean...

"If you guys last after this, you gotta know that she takes everything you say or do to heart, Jay. And God only knows what mental state she's gonna be in after this whole ordeal is over." He put his hand on his forehead and sighed. "You have to be careful. She's very fragile." He looked at me once more and walked back into the house.

CHAPTER TWENTY-TWO
AM'RAK

A m'rak sat at a bar in Baltimore waiting on Mercer to come inside. When he finally got there, three hours late, Am'rak got into his shit. "Fuck took you so long, nigga?"

"I was...I had some things to do." He sat next to him and flagged the bartender. "But I'm here now." The bartender walked over. "I'll take a Corona."

"Did you meet with the dude?"

"Yeah." He took a large gulp of beer when the bartender brought it back.

"Were the police still following you?"

"Yes."

He smiled.

"But, Am'rak, I mean, how you sure this shit gonna work?" Mercer continued. "I know you been working on her for a minute but, the amount of money you dropped and the amount of time you spending on ole girl, how you know they gonna buy it?"

"Because they see what they want to see. And after Juicy from New York got caught last week, they ain't looking for a nigga. She's our way out."

204   BLACK AND THE UGLIEST

Mercer nodded and Am'rak felt uncomfortable with his attitude.

"She's your aunt's way out too right?" Mercer said.

Am'rak frowned at him. "Are you still talking to that bitch you met? The one who knew the niggas who kicked in my front door?"

"What?" Mercer frowned. "Nah! I'm not..." He took a large gulp of his beer. "Ain't nobody thinking 'bout that broad."

Am'rak pointed into his chest with a stiff finger. "Good, you better not. Ain't no room for romance. We on some other shit now."

Am'rak sat on the bed with a bottle of champagne in one hand and a glass in the other. Every so often he would pour the liquid into the flute until he abandoned the glass all together by tossing it on the bed and drinking out the spout.

Parade stood at the foot of the bed wearing a black long designer dress, with jewelry around her neck. Bags of clothes, similar in expense, sat on the floor awaiting her approval. After all, Am'rak spared no expense to make her look 'the part', whatever that meant.

Parade on the other hand was in another world. Her eyes, now a regularly beet red due to constantly crying from missing her family, were a wreck. He smiled at her in awe and understanding. "I can see why every man in the room would want you."

"Why do you want me?"

He laughed. "Didn't I already tell you that I'll let you know when the time is right?"

She looked down at the diamond rings on her fingers. "I feel like you're...you're preparing me for slaughter."

He laughed and stood up. "Why would you say a thing like that?"

"I don't know," she paused. "But is it, is it true?"

He kissed her lips, placed his thumb on the lowest part of her chin and pushed downward. Her mouth opened and he poured champagne down her throat until she almost choked.

Wiping her mouth with the back of her hand she looked up at him. "I would do anything, anything at all for a date."

He guzzled from the bottle and sat on the edge of the bed. "A date for what?"

"For when this will all be over."

He laughed. "You have the world and still it's not enough."

"I'm a married woman. Who loves her family very – "

"Nah, you a whore who I found on an app trying to sell her body. Remember? That's what you told me. And you are a whore to a nigga who deserves everything he's going to get and more."

She lowered her brows. "What does that mean?"

He smiled.

She walked closer, still careful to give him his space. "What does that mean, Am'rak?" She paused. "Jay has never done anything to you."

"Are you sure 'bout that? The past has a way of coming back to haunt you."

She stumbled backward and he stood up. Placing the bottle on the dresser next to the bed, he opened a drawer and pulled out a bag complete with a needle and heroin.

"This is the best product I offer on the streets." He smiled. "Got people willing to sell their souls for it."

"Why are you – "

He slapped her silent. "My mother used this the day she hung herself after losing her fiancé, my father." He looked at it. "You asked me about a date so let me say this. I will never, ever, let you go before I'm finished. And I will never, ever, give you the satisfaction of thinking I will." He handed the bag to her. "Now you can use this as an escape to make yourself feel better. Or you can use this as a ticket to take your own life." He pressed his thumb on two tears that rolled down her face. "The choice is up to you."

She looked at him closer. She had seen the man many times but now he looked very different. Not only was his sinister spirit on full flow, but he also had a familiar face that she could not place.

"This is my life forever," she said in defeat.

"Now you understand."

Parade flopped on the edge of the bed and looked at the drugs. The old her, who lived in L.A. and was successful, would've never considered the thought of getting high again. But having lost her family and finally feeling in her heart that this was certain, she wanted to be somewhere else, even if it was hell.

She looked up at him. "Can you do it for me?" She held out the bag.

His jaw twitched.

Part of him was disgusted that he managed to break her down to the level of wanting to use drugs. And yet the part that planned this moment rejoiced because things were going accordingly.

"Take off your dress."

She stood up and removed her gown. Sitting back on the bed completely naked, he sat next to her. "I finally get his weakness. You are very beautiful."

Confused at his statement, she responded by nodding, as more tears rolled down her face. She held out her arm, veins toward the ceiling and waited. It took him a moment but after a while the needle moved toward her arm like a dripping penis, eager to penetrate her flesh.

Before long it's tip had made contact and he slowly pushed the liquid into her body. Parade's head dropped backwards as she slowly released any emotions not conducive to that moment from her mind. She thought of no husband. No kids. No friends. No life. The only thing that mattered in that second was how good she fucking felt.

When he was done, he slid out the needle. A puddle of blood rested in the pit of her arm. She fell back, face up, feet dangling off the side of the bed.

"Nothing matters," she said to herself.

He smiled, pushed down his jeans, released his dick and climbed on top of her. "Nothing matters now." He slipped into her pussy, moving slowly, savoring every moment. "But all will matter soon." He moved faster when her body juiced up due to the ecstasy she was feeling off the drug. "Trust me, it will matter soon."

AM'RAK

Parade stood in the middle of the living room, dressed in a designer one-piece red dress with diamonds on her neck and fingers. She was waiting on Am'rak to come downstairs. After shooting up last night she was groggy but realized the last thing she needed was to anger him.

When Am'rak finally revealed himself at the top of the steps, he was texting on his phone. Wearing a white t-shirt and grey sweatpants that showcased his big dick print she knew off the top that he wasn't going with her. They looked as if they were in route to two different events.

"The car is out front," Am'rak said as he continued to text. "All you gotta do is drive to the address I gave you."

She nodded. "So you aren't coming with me?"

"Nah, but like I told you before, I always have someone following precious packages and people." He winked. "So you won't be alone." He finally looked at her after the warning. "You look sexy too."

"I feel overdressed." She looked down at herself.

"How could you feel that way when you have no idea where you going?"

BLACK AND THE **UGLIEST**

She nodded. "I guess you're right."

"I am." He paused. "Anyway, don't stop until you get there and then come right back. Don't forget," he pointed at her. "My people know where your folks live in L.A. and where your kids go to school. All this can go badly if you don't follow directions."

She sighed. "Can I get another…you know?"

He frowned." Already hooked huh?"

"Please." She begged.

He shook his head and walked away. When he returned he had the case with heroin and needles in hand. He gave it to her. "Do it before you pull out and then go. I'll see you soon."

Parade nodded and walked out the door. When she was gone he made a call. "Mercer, she's on the way. Them folks still at the location?"

"They sure are," he said.

"Good," he smiled. "If they follow her its all over. Everything falling into place."

CHAPTER TWENTY-THREE
JAY

I was sitting in the parking lot of Quinn's job with Danny hoping the nigga Mercer would show up and we'd get some more info on where he rests his head. We got here at 8:00 am and now it's 10:00 am and still nothing.

"When did you know Parade was the one?" Danny asked me.

I took a deep breath, not really feeling like reminiscing or talking about my personal life. "It took a minute."

"Why?"

I shrugged and leaned back in the passenger's seat, careful to keep my eyes on look out. "Parade wasn't exactly my type at first."

Danny nodded as if he understood.

"What that mean?" I asked.

He frowned. "What you talking about?"

"I told you she wasn't my type and you nodded." I paused. "It's like you being slick or something."

He laughed. "My man, all I did was nod in understanding. There was no maliciousness behind anything, trust me."

I sighed. "My bad."

"All I'm doing is trying to start a conversation because we been in this rental car for hours, probably gonna be here a little longer and I figured the least we could do was get to know each other. You might even realize you like me."

I looked over at him. "Who said I didn't like you?"

"Well at the very least I know you have a problem with gay men. Maybe you think I'll try to make a move on you or—"

"I ain't worried 'bout that."

"Then what is it?"

I focused on Quinn's building again. "I had a close friend in high school. I mean, we did everything together. If there was trouble we probably had something to do with it and I thought I knew everything about him." I sighed deeper, not believing I was even sharing this story. I hadn't even told my wife because I was too embarrassed.

"Well what happened?" Danny asked with wide eyes.

"One night we were over his girl's house. She had the place to herself. So she called her friend and we were both fucking them in his girl's bedroom. She had twin beds so I had one and he had the other. Anyway her mother came home early and we hid in the closet. Naked. Wasn't even able to get our clothes because it happened so quickly. And this nigga…I mean….never mind."

"Man, it's obvious you wanna get it off your chest. Might as well tell me what happened."

I sighed. "We in the closet, with nothing but our socks on holding our dicks when he said, *'I can finish you off if you want.'* I mean, I laughed at first thinking he was joking but he didn't say nothing else. No, *I'm just joking* or, *I'm just playing* or any of that. We spent the next six hours in a dark closet waiting on her mother to leave back out. Not saying a word to each other. Shit was crazy."

"Sorry about that, man."

"That's not the worst part." I paused. "I started ignoring him at school and one day he didn't come back. I figured he'd be out until he could get over the embarrassment but nah, that didn't happen." I took a deep breath. "He hung himself in his mother's closet with a note around his neck that said, *I'm sorry.*"

I looked at him.

"And I always felt like that shit was my fault but at the same time I was mad at him too," I continued. "Mad he put me in that situation and mad he didn't keep that shit to himself."

"It's hard to deny who you really love, man," Danny said.

"Yeah, well, he should've left me out of it," I snapped. "To this day I hate seeing men together because it reminds me of him."

"Maybe that's something you should get over."

I glared just as my phone rang. It was Quinn. I answered and she said, "Do you see that white Tesla?" I squinted until I saw it way on the other side of the parking lot. "That's him."

"She said he over there," I told Danny who nodded.

"He's calling me now," Quinn said. "I gotta go."

Mercer laughed as he talked to Quinn on the phone. Ever since he saw her he was feeling her and now that he had a chance to get to know her more he was falling deeper. Yeah, he knew Am'rak would flip out if he ever thought he was keeping time with her. But the way he saw it, he was his own man so he had to make his own decisions.

"You keep acting like you feeling a nigga and I'ma start believing you." Mercer said.

Quinn looked out the window at him and waved. "I am feeling you but...I mean..."

"What is it?" Mercer grew serious as he looked up at her.

"How come you never get out to see me when you pull up to my job? It's bad enough you pop up whenever you want. The least you could do is formally say hi."

"You don't want me to pop up no more?"

"I'm not saying that," she said quickly. "It's just that, I want to get to know you but I can't get in touch with you unless you reach out to me and I don't know anything 'bout you."

"I know this is crazy." He paused. "I do. But for now it's all I can offer. But if you can hang in there, I'm sure I can make it worth your liking. I promise."

"Well I have to go." She said.

He nodded and hung up without saying bye, something Quinn was used to by now.

Caught up in a cloud of Quinn, when he pulled off he was unaware that Danny and Jay were following him from behind.

CHAPTER TWENTY-FOUR
AM'RAK

*A*nja straddled Am'rak as she looked down into his eyes in the living room of her apartment. She had been thinking about moving on ever since she found Parade in his bed but as always he managed to bring her back.

"I know you tired of waiting but this is kinda your fault," he said seriously.

She frowned. "My fault?"

"Yeah, had I not been trying to catch you fucking for money when – "

"You dumped me, Am!" She yelled. "Already told you that. So I had to go back to what I know. How else could I take care of myself?" She shrugged. "I started back working because I thought you didn't want me no more."

"Nah, you started back selling pussy because you wanted money even though I told you I would always take care of you."

Anja got up and sat next to him. "I don't get it. I mean, what is your thing with her anyway?"

"It's a long story," he said. "Let's just say that we have history and more than that I need her to get me out of a situation."

"Do you love her?"

"Not even close." He paused. "And for now that's all I can say." He looked away and then at her again. "I'll also add this...she took something from me but when this is all said and done she'll give me more and I won't have to play the games anymore."

"Am'rak, I really hope that's true." She said.

"She's nothing like you." He stood up and walked toward the door. "I left you some money on the table in your room. But don't let me catch you on that app again. Or we really over." He walked out.

AM'RAK

Parade packaged the last bag of heroin with her fingers when Am'rak walked up to her in the kitchen at the house down south. She thought it was odd that he didn't want her to use gloves but he was all about keeping her in the dark. And she was all about making him relaxed.

"You done?"

She nodded.

"You look high too." He glared.

"I did a little something before you came," she paused. "I'm fine now though."

He sat at the table and looked at everything. "Put it in the bags." He pointed at the floor to the sacks that were waiting. "You gotta drop them off later."

When his phone beeped he took it out of his pocket and looked at the number. It was from one of the many burners that he used and threw away when done. He made a quick text and then put the phone on the table, wiping his hand down his face. He was visibly irritated.

"I gotta take a shower."

"Everything okay?"

He glared. "You a junkie and you asking if shit fine?" He shook his head and stood up. "Fuck out of here and put my stuff in the sacks like I told you. You gotta make that run." He stormed upstairs.

Parade immediately fulfilled the order and when she looked up and saw the phone was still on the table her heart thumped. This was her big break. Wasting no time, she picked it up and dialed a number. The first voice she heard caused her to cry softly until she slammed her own hand over her mouth.

Removing it slowly she said, "Landon, I miss you." She cried harder. "So much. How...how are you and your brother?"

"We fine, ma but where are you?" He said as he started to cry too. "When you coming home?"

"I don't know. I — "

That quickly Parade had been slapped down to the floor. In her angst to talk to her family she was careless. After striking her hard, Am'rak picked up the phone and hung up before throwing it across the room. Next he grabbed her hair and with a closed fist pounded her face several times.

"Please," she begged with a mouthful of blood. "No....no more."

But Am'rak was relentless. Parade went against the grain even after he forbade her not too so he made her pay. Normally he would've been more careful but he thought the drugs would subdue her a little and make her more submissive. Besides, it happened to his mother when his father left her as a child.

He saw it with his own eyes.

The news that he received earlier on the phone that the cops had still been asking about his aunt fucked up his mind. He had been placing Parade in locations he knew the cops visited hoping that they would think she was in charge. This was another reason he wanted drug residue on her hands, knowing full well it would be in her blood if the cops ever picked her up. But nothing seemed to work. They weren't making the drug Queen Pin and Parade connection.

T. STYLES   221

He had plans to shower, beat his dick and take a nap but now Parade had given him an avenue for his anger and so he took his rage out on her.

In the worst way.

CHAPTER TWENTY-FIVE
JAY

Mercer finally agreed to meet Quinn at a hotel after all this fucking time. And to make sure I could see and hear what was going on we rented two rooms that connected from the bedroom. The plan was simple. He would come over and when he went to the bathroom I would slip into the closet and try and catch any clues I could hear that would lead to my wife.

As open as he was for her I was sure my plan would work.

After he left her job a few days ago we followed him to a condo but he didn't lead us to the dude who had Parade. It was time to change things up. And I'm not gonna lie, I was feeling desperate.

"Listen, when he comes don't act weird," I said to her in the bedroom. "Just be yourself. Smile, laugh at his jokes and whatever—"

"Jay, I may be crazy when it comes to you but I'm still a woman." She smiled. "I know how to talk to dudes."

I sat down on the bed and looked up at her. "I'm sorry."

"You don't gotta be sorry." She sat next to me. "I'm just happy I can do this for you."

I nodded. She said that already. Actually she said it all the time which creeped me out. "I treated you fucked up when you left the hospital and now...now I'm putting you in a situation where I need your help. Talk about karma."

"Jay, I'm not gonna lie, it hurt when you first told me you didn't want anything to do with me but then something changed."

"What?"

"I imagined that you were my husband and you were trying to fight for my return. I mean, she's lucky and I just hope I'll find someone to fight for me the way you do for Parade." She ran her fingers through my curly hair and then dropped her hands in her lap. "Big head."

"You the one with the big ass head," I joked.

"Me?" She pointed to herself while giggling. "I don't even know how you carry that—"

KNOCK. KNOCK. KNOCK.

We both jumped up and I moved to the connecting door. "Lock this when I leave because I know this type dude and he's gonna check it. And when he goes to the bathroom he's gonna check it again. But unlock it right before you go to bed for the night and he takes off his clothes. I'll slip inside after that."

KNOCK. KNOCK. KNOCK.

"I got it, I got it," she said pushing me out. "Now go."

I walked into the other room and waited patiently.

Quinn walked to the door and opened it with a smile. In the moment she was scared. He was glaring, hands inside the large grey sweatshirt he was wearing. "What took you so long?"

"Was in the bathroom?" She frowned. "Why? Are you —"

He pushed inside and ran through the hotel room. He looked in the closets, under the beds and even in the bathroom and shower. When he saw the adjoining room door he glared at her.

"What?"

Without waiting he opened the adjoining door but was met with another door that led to the other room. He twisted the knob but it wouldn't open.

"What's wrong, Mercer?" She asked sitting on the bed. "You making me feel uncomfortable."

"My bad." He took a deep breath. "I guess I got trust issues." He removed his sweatshirt and the gun that was inside and placed it on the chair in the room. The one next to him. "Listen, I'm sorry. The last thing I want is to put you on edge."

Just seeing the gun caused her immediate fright but she kept it together. Besides, Jay was near. For some reason it wasn't until that moment that she realized how serious things really were.

"I don't want anything from you," she said. "You don't have to be so suspicious around me."

He nodded. "I'm sorry. I...I think I'm falling in love with you."

Her heart jumped. "I'm falling for you too," she lied.

"Good, because I've killed before. Even took out a dirty cop at my man's house who was trying to do surveillance on him a few weeks back. I know I just gave you a lot but it's important that you know to never cross me. Because if I killed police, I won't have a problem killing anybody."

She smiled awkwardly. "Hungry?" She swallowed the lump in her throat.

He nodded.

"We could do pizza or...?"

"Let's do Chinese." He paused. "Need some rice." He exhaled, grabbed his gun and pointed to the bathroom with his thumb. "I be back."

She smiled although horrified and called a local delivery service. Since she didn't know what he wanted she ordered large portions of the black folk classic, beef and broccoli and chicken and broccoli with sides of fried rice.

When he came out, just as Jay said, he tried the door again to the adjoining room. When he still couldn't get in he shrugged and said, "It's the hood nigga in me I guess."

"Look, if you don't trust me just leave, Mercer." She stood up and moved near the door. "I don't have time for this because all I'm trying to do is love you and you making me feel dumb for it."

He looked down. "I'm sorry. Please, please don't feel that way. I been fucked up for so long and it's been awhile since somebody wanted to really deal with a nigga. You know?"

"Are you sure?"

"Yeah." He extended his hand. "Let's enjoy the rest of the night." She rolled her eyes and walked over to him.

Grabbing his hand he slowly pulled her into his lap. "What you order?"

"Beef and broccoli and chicken with rice."

He smiled. "Damn, you know me."

She giggled.

Three hours later his guard was down and they were in bed kicking shit. Feeling like things were good, when he went to the bathroom again she unlocked the door. Jay slid inside the room and walked into the closet across from the bed, something Quinn didn't realize he was going to do.

Now she wanted to shit her thong because he was so near but she had to be more relaxed. When Mercer walked out the bathroom he looked at the adjoining door but this time moved straight for the bed. She breathed an invisible sigh of relief. "So, tell me some stuff about yourself?" She asked him. "Where you work?"

He looked at her funny. "You really are green aren't you?"

She frowned. "I'm not from the streets but I'm not green either." She said softly. "But why you say that?" She crawled on top of him, straddled him and looked down at his face.

"I don't know," he shrugged looking up at her. "To me what I do and who I am is obvious."

"I still don't get it."

He laughed lightly. "And I don't want you to either. I want to keep safe any idea you have of me in your mind. Just know that I'm a hood nigga. And sometimes I do hood nigga things."

"I like you," she said.

"Oh yeah," he winked.

"Yeah."

When she felt him stiffening she rose up a little and inserted him inside her pussy. "That's better. You're more comfortable in there."

"Whoa," Mercer said as he felt her juicy tight pussy. "And this thing is right too." He bit his bottom lip.

"I'm not for everybody." She paused. "Don't believe in ruining my body for just any nigga. Ain't nobody breaking down the walls of this pussy."

He nodded. "I know that."

Wanting to hear more of what was being done and said, Jay opened the closet door just to see a little. He was fine with listening from the inside but when they started fucking their voices were too low. The moment he opened the door and he saw Quinn bucking them yellow hips back and forth, his dick stiffened.

No he wasn't thinking about being with her on the official tip. But he didn't see nothing wrong with thinking about how good the pussy was, especially since he was sure his wife was putting out too.

After Quinn and Mercer finished, Mercer got dressed and kissed her after his phone rang with a call from Am'rak.

"Before you leave I want to say something, Mercer. I'm sorry about that thing with that dude," she said. "I didn't know he was going to break into your friend's house. And I'm glad you still trust me."

He nodded. "Can't lie, it was pretty fucked up," he paused. "Am'rak be tripping sometimes which is why I can't let him know about you."

She smiled and kissed him again. "Can't wait to see you later. When you have time for me."

He didn't say a word and Jay understood. He had that same feeling when he was with Parade in the beginning. Where you already gone but you trying to hold it together.

Jay may not have found out anything additional through Mercer other than Am'rak's name but he was reminded of how fine Quinn was.

When Quinn walked Mercer to the door and returned, Jay was sitting on the edge of the bed waiting. "Good job." He clapped. "Outstanding actually."

She sensed sarcasm in his voice. "How was it good?" She said flopping next to him. "We don't know nothing else other than Am'rak's name."

He looked at her closely.

"What, Jay?"

"Did you like fucking him? Because it looked like you had a good time." He joked.

"That performance was for you. Since I knew you were watching."

He shook his head. "Go 'head with that shit."

She got on her knees between his legs and unleashed his dick. "That was for you, Jay." She ran her tongue on the side of his stiffness. "But now here's the ending." She inhaled him before he could say no.

CHAPTER TWENTY-SIX
JAY

I overslept in the hotel with Quinn and guilt rocked me to the core. Why the fuck I let that girl suck my dick? And it wasn't like I wasn't thinking about Parade in order to bust a nut either.

On the ride back to her house she kept smiling and touching my thigh and shit. I didn't have the heart to tell her that nothing changed with me. Or that being with her was the first time I'd touched a woman in years other than my wife.

I had a moment of weakness.

The second we walked through the door Wayne was standing in front of it with his arms crossed over his body. "Where were you?" He asked Quinn and then me. "Why are you just getting back now?"

Quinn looked at him, smiled and walked to her bedroom.

I took a deep breath because Quinn left me alone. "We couldn't leave right away." I crossed my arms over my chest then dropped them at my sides. For some reason I couldn't get comfortable. Maybe it was the hard way he was looking at me. "We needed to make sure the coast was clear."

"Jay Hernandez!" He yelled. "Your ass is lying."

I walked away and flopped on the sofa.

"Did you fuck that girl?" Wayne continued.

"Nah."

"You lying."

"Listen, you not my mother or my wife so I don't owe you no explanation. Now I said I didn't fuck the girl and you gonna have to believe it or not."

"Well while you were out doing I don't know what, Parade called." He said.

I jumped up and approached him. "Called who? Called where?"

"Your son. Landon." He walked away and headed to the kitchen. I followed closely behind him.

"Well what did she say?" I felt like I was about to hit the floor. Fuck was I thinking posting up with this broad when I was here for my wife? "Did she...did she tell him where she was? Did she...I mean..."

"She didn't get a chance to say anything because he must've hit her." Wayne opened the refrigerator and grabbed some orange juice and then a glass from the cabinet.

I snatched the jug from him and slammed it on the counter. "What happened to her?"

"I TOLD YOU ALL I FUCKING KNOW!" He yelled. "AND IF YOU CARED SO MUCH YOU WOULD HAVE BEEN HERE INSTEAD OF RUNNING AROUND WITH THAT BITCH! NOW GET THE FUCK OUTTA MY FACE!" He stormed off.

As mad as I was that I wasn't there to talk to my son or find out more information Wayne was right. I shouldn't have been in a hotel letting Quinn suck my dick. I should've been on guard to make sure I was able to receive any call that Parade placed and now…I mean…everything is all fucked up.

Later on that day I called my son and got as much information as I could but he pretty much said what Wayne said, that Parade was cut off before she could say much of anything.

After speaking to my kids and asking Adrian if he needed anything to care for them, I walked to Quinn's bedroom where she was folding clothes. The moment she saw me she rushed over to me, grabbed my hands and closed the door and turned the lock.

I walked inside and sat on the edge of the bed. "I owe you an apology, Quinn."

She shook her head. "No, no, no," she sat next to me. "Please don't do this to me."

"I'm not doing anything to you."

She sat closer. "Jay, we had a good time last night. And we had a nice time this morning over breakfast. I don't care if I'm the other woman. Just as long as I can be in your life some kind of way and —"

"I didn't come back to Maryland to have a relationship outside of my wife." I walked away. "I came here so I could find her. And I know it's fucked up but I got caught up in the drama and…"

"You fucked me." She cried. "Wow. I feel so stupid."

My hand hovered over her shoulder because as her head hung I wanted to touch her and tell her I was sorry. I wanted to comfort her because how I acted was foul but I knew if I gave her one-ounce of love she would read things the wrong way.

"I didn't fuck you. I let you suck my dick. There's a difference."

I got up, walked toward the door and looked back once before going out. The moment I was on the other side of it Danny was waiting. He frowned and said, "What's wrong with Quinn? Is she in there crying?"

"A long story, man."

T. STYLES   235

"Well walk with me out back. I have to talk to you."

When we walked outside he took a deep breath. "I have a plan to get Parade back. It's putting things on the line for me but it's worth it."

My eyes widened. "Don't play with me, Danny. For real I'm not in the mood."

"You know I wouldn't do that." He paused. "This is serious. But I'm gonna need you to do some things to make this work."

"Anything."

"You have to convince Quinn you feeling her," he paused. "Because she's a huge part of the plan. And it may mean her life."

Fuck.

JAY

I was in the back of a movie theater with Quinn feeling like a chump. Had I not let her give me head before everything went south then I might not have to

BLACK AND THE UGLIEST

do so much. But now I was in another bind and after speaking to Danny I realized she was our answer and a necessary part to bring Parade home.

After the movie I took her to a small restaurant where people wouldn't recognize me and focused. "Listen, Quinn, I wanna apologize again."

She smiled as she ate a fry. "Apologize or make up?" She asked placing her other hand on my thigh.

"Come on, Q."

She yanked her hand away. "Jay, what's going on? You said you were sorry and then brought me out and now you tripping again. I can't with all the mental games."

When someone walked toward us and dropped something on the floor, we both jumped. "Sorry about that," the stranger said before picking up his wallet and walking away.

Everything made me nervous being out and I definitely needed to get back to her house but she wasn't smoothed over enough yet.

"I realize I do want something with you," I lied. "But I can't put names on our relationship right now. Is that good enough?"

She nodded her head up and down and smiled. "That's all I was asking for. I know you made vows. I just want a place with you that's all."

I took a deep breath. Next I picked up my cell and placed it to my ear as if someone called. "Oh yeah, okay, I'll let you know. Yeah, I'm out with her right now." I winked at Quinn. "Cool." I fake hung up and sipped my beer. I needed her to ask who was on the phone first instead of coming at her crazy to complete my plan.

"Who was that?" She asked.

Yes! I thought.

"Danny." I said. "He said he has a plan for Mercer." I paused. "I'm glad."

"Why you say that?"

"To be honest I was starting to think nothing would go as planned so I'm happy to hear that something is in the works."

"What does he have in mind?" She asked with wide eyes. "I mean, did he give you the details or did he just tell you about having a plan?"

"Wait, you still wanna help?" I paused. "Because you haven't really said anything about Parade since we left the hotel and —"

"Jay, if you in the picture I'm in the picture too." She said smiling. "Especially now since I'm a part of your world. I mean, you did so much today to prove that you care and that's all I wanted. Now I feel like, like, you give a fuck and...well...I just want to say thank you that's all."

I knew it. She was basically saying that if I didn't give her a place in my life then she wouldn't help me find my wife. That's what I can't stand about some females. They connect one thing that doesn't have anything to do with the other when they mad.

"You know I care about you, Quinn." I drank some of my beer since the lie tasted like shit in my mouth. "But I need to take care of business so my mind can be clear first. You get that?"

"I get that." She said. "So um, what's the plan? I mean if you don't mind me asking."

I sat up and clasped my hands in front of me on the table. She was falling right into our trap. "We need you to call Mercer and get him to be at a certain location."

She frowned. "What you mean?"

"He just needs to be at a location we set up."

She sat back. "So how can I get him there?" She paused. "I mean you saw how suspicious he was when he came to the hotel room. An open place will probably make him snap on me."

"I know but we need this. And I also understand that it's dangerous but, well, if you don't go I'll never get Parade back."

Suddenly she had a look in her eyes that made my stomach shift. It was almost as if she was considering not helping so that Parade would never come home. "I want to help, Jay," she said softly. "Honestly."

"Good, because if she not back I'm not gonna be right in the head." I put the truth out there so that if she even thought about us running off in the sunset she would have to think again. "Shit not gonna be cool with me. You get what I'm saying?"

"Yes," she nodded rapidly. "We'll bring her back. You'll see."

JAY

Me, Wayne and Danny were seated at the table with Quinn at the house. Tonight was the night to move forward to put an end to the games and find my

BLACK AND THE UGLIEST

wife. Besides, Wayne was told by the friends he has watching over our kids that Logan was spending more time at his girl's and that Landon was having trouble dealing with Ella because she was too mouthy. It was time for me to return to L.A. with my wife and put shit back in order. It was time for all of us to head back.

"Remember to sound hysterical," I told Quinn.

"But what if he doesn't come?" She asked looking at me and then Danny and Wayne. "What if...what if..."

"Listen, suga, he's called you every other hour since leaving you at the hotel right?" Wayne asked her.

I wasn't even aware of that but it was good to hear.

"Yeah, I mean..."

"So if he's calling you every hour that means he's feeling you," Wayne continued. "And that means he will come if you sound scared enough. He's desperate to keep you but you have to put everything into the call okay?"

She nodded and then slowly a glare came over her face. "I know yah just using me but whatever."

Here she go with the wacko shit. I thought.

I looked at Wayne and then Danny. This was the last thing we needed right now. Danny and Wayne had already gotten things together on their end and we didn't need her fucking up. I had to take charge or risk her pulling out or even asking us for money depending on how foul she was at the moment.

"You know what," I said. "This why I can't be with you." I got up and walked across the room toward the sofa. I wanted to rock the power she had over us right then. "And you wonder why I left you for Sky." I flopped down. "You know what, fuck it, don't do nothing for me. We'll think of another plan." I was definitely bluffing because although we knew where Mercer stayed, he had yet to lead us to Am'rak.

Quinn jumped up and sat next to me. "No, I was just talking, Jay. You know how I behave sometimes. But I'll do it." She placed her hand on my knee. "I promise."

When I glanced up I saw Wayne sitting with his arms folded tightly across his body. I knew he was heated that she was touching me but I had to give him a look to fall back. That wasn't working and then I sighed in relief when I saw Danny hold Wayne back from snatching her head off.

"I'll call him right now." Quinn got up and grabbed the phone off the table. "I won't let you down, Jay. I promise." She dialed the number and took a deep breath.

I watched impatiently from the sofa.

"Hello," she cried hysterically. "Mercer, it's me." She paused. "Yes, somebody just stole my purse and I need you to pick me up." She cried harder. "Please." She paused and looked at us. "Yes, thank you so much. Thank you." She hung up and wiped the fake tears that rolled down her face. "Was that good enough for you?" She asked.

I nodded yes, but also realized that she had more shit with her than I thought.

MERCER

"Where are you?" Mercer asked on his cell phone. "I got shit to do tonight and I hope you not out here playing games."

When Mercer got off the phone with Quinn's voicemail his line rang again. This time it was Am'rak. "Where you at?"

"I got some errands but I'll be there soon."

"How come you seem out of it lately? Ain't dependable no more?"

Mercer frowned. He was trying his best to respect Am'rak. After all he had done a lot for him and he knew it. Including finding out about Parade's life. At the same time he was pushy and he carried on as if he owned him.

"Am, look, man, I do everything you need me to do. I'm on duty twenty-four seven and even said fuck my life so you could have one."

"Never asked you to do that."

"You didn't have to. At the same time that's how you carry shit if I don't move fast enough." He paused. "Now let me handle my business but trust me when it's time to move I will."

"Just make sure you be watching the spot in an hour," Am'rak said. "I got word that the police finally bit the fake leads we gave them. So I need to put Parade in position."

"I promise I'm on it," Mercer said. "Just make sure she's ready." When his phone rang he looked at it. It was the other line. "I gotta take this." Mercer hung up before he could respond. "Hello," He paused. "Quinn? Where you at?"

"I'm up the street. Can you see me?"

He squinted and saw her waving one block up. He smiled. "Yep, got eyes on you now." He put the car in drive. "I'm on the way."

The moment he pulled in front of her and unlocked the door, two people he didn't see originally slid inside. They were Adrian, Wayne's flamboyant gay friend who took over the front seat while Dayshawn, who although was normally reserved slid in the back. They both were dressed in drag and shimmering.

When Mercer looked at Quinn she ran away.

"Who the fuck are you?" Mercer asked reaching for his gun before Dayshawn held a knife to his throat from behind. Adrian noticed and took the gun from inside Mercer's waist.

"We just looking for a ride, baby boy," Dayshawn said. "Ain't no need in dying over it."

"So this a set up?" Mercer asked, as he plotted against Quinn in his mind.

"Set up?" Adrian laughed. "Chile, we saw you alone and needed a ride. I don't know what all else you talking about." He said, trying to spare Quinn any additional trauma that would probably come her way. "Now do us a favor and ride."

"Where?"

"Away from here," Dayshawn said looking out the window behind him. "We got people looking for us and the last thing we wanna do is sit around."

"Listen, I can't — "

Dayshawn jabbed the knife into his side, pricking his flesh. "You can and you will." He said through clenched teeth. "Now go."

Angry with the world, Mercer drove up the street even though they didn't give him a firm address. Despite it all, the only thing he was worried about was Quinn and if she would be okay. He no longer felt like she set him up.

They were a mile up the road when suddenly an unmarked police car pulled up behind him. "Oh no!" Dayshawn yelled looking back at the flashing lights. "They fucking caught up with us."

"Who is it?" Mercer asked frantically, although knowing full well it was the police. "And what ya'll got me into? I ain't got nothing to do with yah niggas!"

"Just keep driving!" Adrian demanded. "And don't let him catch us."

"I'm not gonna keep driving." He pulled over. Besides, it wasn't like he had drugs in his ride. "You crazy?" He cut the car off and tucked the keys in his pocket. "Fuck this shit. You gonna have to shoot me or something."

"They gonna lock us up!" Adrian acted.

"You?" Dayshawn screamed. "I'm the one they looking for!"

"Wait?" Adrian said. "Why you the one?"

"License and registration," Danny said approaching the driver's side of the car with extreme authority, flashlight shining directly into Mercer's face.

"I can give you that, sir," Mercer said softly. "But before I do I just want you to know that I have nothing to do with these niggas in here. I was waiting on my girl and they – "

"License and registration!" Danny snapped.

Mercer nervously collected the documents and gave him what he asked for. When Danny reviewed them he flashed a light into the car on Adrian and Dayshawn who struck a pose. Danny secretly felt Adrian was doing too much by living up to gay stereotypes but who cared? They flew in town when called upon. Being available helped the bottom line.

"And who are you two?" Danny asked Adrian and Dayshawn.

"You know who I am." Dayshawn said. "You locked me up enough times already."

Danny smirked. "I just want to hear the words," Danny said.

"I was trying to make a little money okay?" Dayshawn shrugged. "A working girl's gotta earn even if it is selling bussy." He rubbed Mercer's shoulder and he violently knocked it away.

Mercer's eyes widened. "Wait...this isn't what it looks like, sir. I don't know why he in here lying but – "

"And what does it look like?" Danny asked.

"That I'm...that..."

"You're picking up two male prostitutes," Dayshawn said finishing his sentence.

"Yes, but they jumped into my car without me knowing and – "

"That's what they all say," Danny said. "But I do know this," he paused. "You're gonna be the laughing stock around the precinct when I book your ass tonight. Just hope your friends find it as amusing as I do."

Just thinking about his reputation and how damaged it would be put him on the immediate path to a panic attack. Am'rak's response alone was enough to make him go crazy. "Please don't lock me up," Mercer said. "I'm begging you."

"This nigga in here acting like it's the worst thing to be caught buying bussy from us," Adrian said to Mercer. "If you would try us a little you'd know we the best in the business."

"I don't want no parts of this shit," Mercer snapped at them both. "Now stop fucking around before I go off on you!" He looked back at Danny and took a deep breath. "Please, officer. Don't take me back to the precinct with them. I'm willing to do anything."

Danny shined the light on his face. "Anything?"

"Just say the word."

CHAPTER TWENTY-SEVEN
JAY

We had Mercer tied up in the basement of Danny's aunt's house. She lived alone and barely went downstairs so we knew it was the perfect location to question him more. At the moment the plan wasn't to hurt him. I just wanted to find out where Parade was and to make sure she was okay.

The problem was I couldn't trust myself. Just thinking about her being affiliated with these niggas made me more than jealous.

It made me psychopathic.

To help out with our plan Danny had his two cousins Brad and Daley with us. They were a couple of dudes who didn't have lives outside of the streets but would jump at the chance for trouble. Still, they seemed to respect Danny and that's all I needed.

Mercer was tied up to a wooden chair while me and Danny stood in front of him. The moment Mercer saw my face he shook his head. I guess everything made sense now and he knew he had to come clean. At least I hoped so.

"Where is she?" I asked plainly.

"I can't help you with that," he rolled his eyes and looked away.

Brad, the biggest of Danny's cousin's went upside his face with a whip stick, which ripped into the flesh of his cheek. Danny was mad that his cousin reacted so crazy so he shoved him away.

I smiled, especially when Mercer started talking. Can't lie. Mercer took me as the type to hold on to Intel but apparently he was pretty weak. "Listen, I don't know where he took her, man."

"How come I don't believe you?" I asked. "You be with the nigga everyday."

Mercer frowned, blood running down his eye. "How you know that?" He paused. "Huh? You don't know nothing about me or the niggas I roll with. You fresh out the hospital bed anyway."

"I'm asking the questions around here," I said. I was trying to throw him off of Quinn's track because I didn't want her harmed after all this. "Now where the fuck is my wife?"

"I don't know."

This time I hit him after snatching the whip stick from Brad's hand. I went upside the other side of his face with as much force as I could. "WHERE THE FUCK IS SHE!" Danny pushed me back but I shoved him across the room as I approached Mercer again. "I'm not gonna ask you no more. I promise."

Mercer, whose head was hung low and bloody took several deep breaths and looked up at me. "There are some things you don't know about Am'rak. He ain't the kind of person who tells you everything he does so he keeps me on a short leash."

"What does that mean?" Danny asked.

"Ever since he took Parade he been on some other shit. I mean, at first it seemed like he ran into her by accident. Like it was some crazy situational fate type event but now, well now it feels personal."

"Personal?" Danny asked. "For what?"

I scratched the top of my head and moved closer. "And why would Am'rak make things personal to her?"

"Like I said, man I don't know," Mercer shrugged as blood continued to pour down his face. "Do you know Am'rak?"

"Fuck nah."

"Well, he's very secretive. He only tells me what he wants me to know. For the most part he's really close to his aunt who has been the key distributor to a drug dealer in Cuba ever since I was in diapers. She never been found out until recently. The thing is now she's losing her mind a little and making mistakes. Just recently the DEA got a hold of some info that she may be responsible for bringing in work because she told her hairstylist while under the dryer...but I think...I think he may be about to frame Parade as the Queen Pin instead."

I backed up.

"How?" Danny frowned.

"I'm telling you all I know," Mercer continued. "Whatever you do, please don't kill me."

CHAPTER TWENTY-EIGHT
JAY

The moment we got outside his aunt's house Danny pushed me backwards. "Are you crazy?" He asked.

I swung at him but he ducked and missed my blow by inches. "Fuck wrong with you?" I yelled.

"Fuck wrong with me?" He pointed at himself. "I thought the plan was to question him. Not to hurt him. Don't you realize I'm retired and borrowed the car to get info. If something happens to him I'm going to jail!"

"Are you serious?" I asked sarcastically. "These niggas got the woman who gave birth to my kids in some—"

"She had a part in this, Jay." He said. "Let's not forget that Parade willingly kept time with him to get the house back. She wanted to be where she is right now."

"Meaning?"

"I just said it." He paused. "Had Parade not willingly left with them none of this would be happening."

"Danny, for your safety, I suggest you stop talking." I warned. "I'm being all the way serious."

"And so am I."

"Just because she agreed to do whatever she agreed doesn't mean, you know what..." I walked to the car and got inside the passenger seat. Just talking about this shit was sending me on edge and I wasn't trying to hurt ole' boy.

Danny waited a few minutes and then he got in the driver's seat. "First let me say that I want Parade home just as much as you."

"I doubt it but 'aight."

"I'm serious, Jay. If nothing else just to make sure Wayne stays out of this shit because I have a feeling if he doesn't stop coming to your wife's rescue he's gonna kill our marriage and himself."

I nodded. "Listen, if you got a problem with how I handle any of this I suggest you get out the car now. Because it's very important that you know that I intend on seeing this through to the end."

"Just let me talk when we get to his aunt's house okay? Please, man." He looked over at me. "I'm putting my reputation and life on the line." He paused. "Alright?"

I looked out the window. "Let's go."

When we made it to a single-family house with a small garden out front I thought we were at the wrong address. There was no way that anybody who lived here sold drugs. It was a front, and a good one at that.

We walked up to the door and knocked several times. Immediately an elderly woman with white hair that looked like soft cotton opened it. Her skin was as wrinkled as freshly washed sheets and she was wearing a light blue muumuu with a red apron over it. From the scent of cake coming from inside I gauged she was baking.

"Hello, fellas." She smiled. "Can I help you?" She looked up and down the block. "Lost?"

"No," Danny said. "But we are here about possible drug activity in this neighborhood. Actually in your house."

Slowly the smile vanished. In that second I could see the façade she held up for so long wash away. Now she looked like a drug lord. "I told my boy I couldn't go through this and he promised me." She dug into her pocket and texted someone. Next she reached into her other pocket and pulled out a gun.

"Ma'am," Danny said with his hand hovering over his weapon. "Put the gun down. Please! All we wanna do is talk."

She smiled, put it under her chin and blew her brains out. Her innards splattered on me and Danny's faces.

"What the fuck! What the fuck!" Danny kept chanting. "What the fuck! What the fuck!"

I bent down and grabbed the old lady. "I'm going inside to see what I can find out."

"Jay," he grabbed my arm. "We have to leave now, man."

I snatched away from him. "I'm going inside." I dragged her body into the threshold.

Danny placed both of his hands in the air. "I can't deal with this anymore. You know what, Jay, you are officially on your own." He walked off and drove away.

I didn't care. I closed the door behind him and walked through the house for answers. It didn't take me more than a few minutes to find out everything I needed to know from a little red phonebook she kept on her kitchen table next to her house phone. She was definitely sloppy and I'm sure she was making other major mistakes. I knew more about Am'rak in that moment than he probably knew about himself. This woman recorded everything.

It was also clear after I saw some of the names in her book that Parade was in trouble. If they found out that his aunt was dead and that I did it they may try to hurt her in retaliation.

I had to get her away from him now.

DOWN SOUTH (VIRGINIA)
AM'RAK

Am'rak stepped out of the shower preparing to make some runs, only to see Parade lying on the bed asleep. He figured she was high as usual because lately she had been shooting up so much in the bathroom she was barely conscious when he saw her.

At first he was annoyed that she was hitting the bag so hard but with time he started not to care.

Besides, if things went his way tonight she would be arrested as The Queen Pin and his great aunt Quila would be free and clear. But since it was their last night together he figured the least he could do was get a shot of pussy for old times sake.

The moment he slipped in bed he was surprised to see that she was wearing no shirt or bra, only grey sweatpants. "Why you got clothes on girl?" He bit down on his bottom lip. "You normally sleep naked." He slipped behind her since she was lying on her side.

She didn't respond.

"Parade, stop the fake shit. I know you hear me." He pushed down one side of her sweat pants preparing to fuck. "You know you gotta get up in a minute anyway since – "

Before he could respond there was a needle lodged in the side of his neck by Parade. It was filled with all the heroin she had requested from him over the days. She was able to push some into him but when he jumped up she plunged the heroin needle in his back and shot it in him as he tried to get away.

Am'rak thought she stayed high but outside of the first time Parade took a hit, when he inserted it into her arm, she hadn't taken another hit since. Her plan was to make him think that she wasn't aware of life so that he would let his guards down and that's exactly what he did. She knew trying to kill him was dangerous because he could possibly murder her family but she had to take a chance. She even laid out how they would get away from L.A. after they stole more of his money.

"You fucking, bitch!" He yelled from the bathroom. "I'm gonna...I'm gonna kill you."

After causing as much damage as she felt she could, she leapt off the bed and moved toward the stairs. Running down them she tripped and missed the last three steps, falling down to the bottom.

Her legs and arms ached badly but she had to get away. Wearing no shirt, she opened the front door only to see Jay standing in front of her. Thinking she was losing her mind, she backed up into the house.

How could he possibly be there?

"Parade," Jay said with tears in his eyes. "Bae, it's me."

Emotionally battered for days on end she shook her head left and right. "No...no it's not. How, you didn't even know where I was. You..."

He rushed inside and pulled her to him. "Parade, it's me." He gripped her strongly. "I found you."

She looked up at him and cried so hard her body went limp. Exhausted and relieved, she fell into his arms and although Jay himself wasn't one hundred percent on the mend after the accident, he managed to maintain the hold of his wife.

When she was a little calmer he separated from her and said, "Parade, where is dude? This nigga threatened my family and I, I did something I had to do and I gotta kill him before he kills us."

"I killed him already." She wiped tears from her eyes.

He frowned. "You killed him? How?"

"Yes, but, how did you get here?" She looked at him. "And are you okay? Should you be out of the hospital and —"

"I'm 'aight. I took an Impala from this dude's aunt to come get you but we'll get into all that shit later. You remember the nigga Cannon?"

So much was happening but Parade remembered him vaguely. "I, I'm not sure. Why?"

"Parade, he was the dude that Smokes hired to kill you when we lived in the manor." He said. "Back in the day. Don't you remember that shit? He was going to kill you over — "

"A game of Truth or Dare." Her eyes widened. Now everything started to make sense. The similarities in Cannon and Am'rak's facial features were un-canning. She knew he looked familiar but she was a grown woman with three kids and a husband. Miles away from her days back at the Manor so her memory was faulty about the past.

"He's his son, Parade," Jay continued. "And — "

"And it's because of you my father not here!" Am'rak said from the top of the stairs. He was barely holding on but the .45 revolver he had aimed at them made him feel stronger. "I got a text from my aunt, nigga. And don't even think about reaching for a weapon." He slid down one step. Holding the rail with one hand and the gun in the other. "Your wife may have tried to kill me but I still got enough strength to pull this trigger."

"It's over, man," Jay said moving Parade behind him to shield her. "The cops are at your aunt's house right now. I made an anonymous call when I went through the house and saw all the drugs and shit yah were moving on these streets. A little sloppy if you ask me then again you already know. For her to be such a big dealer but whatever," he shrugged. "What I don't get is why you wanted to frame my wife?"

"Are you serious?" He laughed sliding down another step. "This bitch and her friends were the cause of my father having to leave Texas to do a hit. My mother hung herself when he died in prison. Before that she got hooked on heroin after learning he actually fell for that bitch!"

"I'm the one who had somebody kill your father in prison!" Jay corrected him. "Not my wife!"

"I don't give a fuck who did it," he laughed heartedly. "All I know is my life suffered behind this shit. And now we're here." He scooted down one more step.

Suddenly Jay started squinting and Parade noticed as Am'rak moved closer. "What's wrong?" She whispered to Jay.

Jay smiled, pulled out the gun he got from his friend and aimed at Am'rak. Squeezing the trigger he splattered his brains all over the walls behind him. Parade lost her mind.

"WHAT, HOW DID YOU, HOW DID YOU KNOW HE DIDN'T…"

"The chamber wasn't full and I saw only one bullet. I took my chances."

It was then that Parade recognized the gun lying at the foot of the steps. It was the same one he gave her when the dirty cop moved on his house and he killed him.

Suddenly Jay's phone beeped. When he looked down he got the worst message he wanted to see. "What is it?" Parade asked in horror.

"We gotta go now!" They ran out the door.

JAY

The moon was in rare form as it hovered above the filthy, grungy water that made up the Potomac River, causing it to

BLACK AND THE UGLIEST

shine in a liquid blue hue. A little to the right, on a patchy land that Chocolate City called Hains Point, Danny and Wayne stood on their knees, their gaze toward the river.

Their fate unclear.

Standing above them, Mercer aimed the warm barrel of a .45 in their direction, which had already been fired once as a warning shot indicating that he alone was in charge.

After what seemed like an eternity, slowly a black Impala rolled up in the parking lot some ways over from the group, the brightness of the headlights made Mercer squint slightly to see who was arriving. Normally policemen circled the tourist trap but a bomb threat had been called in not even three miles ahead to a government building, which required all available officers on deck.

It was Mercer who made the call.

When the car parked, the lights went out, placing the scene as it was before its arrival.

Dark.

Scary.

Uncertain.

Slowly Parade and Jay eased out, carefully toward the trio.

Observant, Jay glared at Mercer, believing that if he tried hard enough he could knock him to the ground and end this madness once and for all.

"Don't be stupid!" Mercer suggested, aiming at Parade and Jay and then back at Danny and Wayne who were still on their knees. He killed Brad and Daley back at Danny's aunt's house for striking him in the face and was uneasy. Jay thought Danny's cousins could handle him when they left and since Mercer was alive it was evident that they couldn't. "I'm feeling kinda nervous right now. Don't make me kill everybody out this bitch before you have a chance to hear me out."

Jay's hands went up in the air. "I'm unarmed." He paused. "Please don't do anything crazy."

Mercer aimed at Parade. "Me too." She cleared her throat. "Me…me too."

Mercer returned his weapon onto the men on their knees and laughed. "Let me ask yah something right quick."

"I'm listening," Jay said.

"You wouldn't happen to have a little liquor in the ride would you?" He snickered awkwardly. "Seeing as how at least one of you niggas are gonna die today." He laughed hysterically. "We might as well drink to pouring blood."

"Please don't," Parade felt light headed as her words left her mouth. Just thinking about losing Wayne was not an option and would surely bring her as close as possible to a nervous breakdown. "Please don't hurt them. If you're going to hurt anybody hurt me."

"Maybe," Mercer nodded. "I could certainly do that, but this is the mothafucka who pulled over my car and because of it, made me kill Quinn after realizing she had to be involved."

Jay's head rotated quickly toward Parade and then back at Mercer. He felt extreme guilt for Quinn's death but it was all about his wife. "Hey, man, they didn't have nothing to do with us," he said about Danny and Wayne. "Don't do this."

"Why can't I keep anything for myself, huh?" He yelled, spit flying from his mouth. "Why can't I ever be happy? I fucking loved that girl!"

Parade was now crying so hard she could barely see. She couldn't visualize any scenario that would end with them all leaving out safely. And since it was her fault she had to make a move.

So she charged Mercer, throwing him off guard. He expected Jay to try something but this was different. Aiming at her, since she jumped, he decided she could get a bullet first. But Danny seeing this knocked Mercer down with his body and then BOOM.

Parade screamed when she saw their bodies meshed together and Wayne quickly rose and looked at the two. It was difficult to see who was hurt because neither was moving and Danny was on top of Mercer. Afraid, Jay rushed toward them and when Mercer began to move it was obvious that Danny had taken the hit.

Wayne screamed at the top of his lungs as Parade grabbed the weapon. This was the worse that could happen. Danny moaned loudly, the wound causing him extreme pain. Wayne's heart was ripped out in such a violent way.

After kicking Mercer in the gut and head repeatedly, Jay managed to remove his own weapon and shoot Mercer several times in the face. Just that quickly it was all over.

Parade untied Wayne's arms before he rushed to Danny where he suffered a gunshot to the belly.

"I love you," he said to Wayne. "You know that right?"

Wayne rocked him in his arms. "Baby, we gonna get you out of here."

Jay untied Danny's arms, tucked the gun behind his jeans and picked him up, before rushing him to the hospital.

EPILOGUE

The funeral was a disaster.

Wayne, for the first time in his life, was too weak both emotionally and physically to walk. Not even for his husband's funeral and so he had to be pushed in with a wheelchair.

The crowd in and out of the church was massive yet sullen, causing the minister's voice to disappear under the sounds of cries. Some wept because Danny Hurts was truly a good man and other's because witnessing Wayne fall was too much to bear.

Parade fell in with the second group, blaming herself for it all. Her feelings weren't without warrant. Had she never took Am'rak on none of this would've happened.

Wayne had shunned Parade since they'd returned back to L.A. so she was grief stricken. Even having her family safe and sound didn't shield her pain.

But Parade had had enough. She drove to Wayne's house where he was outside, on his knees in his garden planting roses. When he heard a noise he turned around and sighed, before focusing back on his garden again. "Danny was allergic," he said.

"To what?" She asked softly.

"Roses. Plants." He giggled. "Everything honestly." He sighed deeper. "Now that I think about it, he wanted most of my attention on him. Maybe that's why he didn't want me having a hobby. He was always – " Unable to move past the pain, he broke down crying.

Parade rushed up to him but he extended his hand, stopping her from getting closer.

"Wayne," she said passionately. "I miss you. Don't you miss me?"

"You're selfish, Parade." He wiped his tears away with his arm. "And I, I never saw it until recently." He continued potting his flowers.

"But how could you say that? I have always showed you how much I love you."

"You could've gone a different route with all of this. You could've taken my advice and gone a different way, Parade. You could've stayed by Jay's side in the hospital and then my Danny would still be alive."

"You made a choice!" Parade yelled, fists clenched tightly. "I never asked you to but you made it all the same!"

Wayne smiled and rose while facing her. "There you go, honey. Reveal yourself, Parade Knight." He walked toward her. "Little Miss Selfish One."

Guilt stricken she dropped to her knees at his feet. "Wayne, I'm sorry. I shouldn't have given that gun back to you that you gave me. Then I could've – "

"None of what should have happened will bring back Danny, his cousins or his aunt."

"I'm so fucking sorry! But I can't live like this...I need you back in my life. Please."

He looked down at her. "You're spoiled and it's part my fault. I tried to show you that the difference in your skin color made you worthy of love no matter what, but you believed it made you a victim."

"Wayne, I...I..." She was so hysterical she could hardly form words or catch her breath and still there were so many things left to be said. "I was lost. I didn't, I didn't know what to do." She paused. "I even prayed to God and got no help."

"He answered you," Wayne yelled. "Through me. Through Bianca who wanted to go into business with you and through Sirena who had enough room for you and your family to live in one of her apartment buildings. And instead of hearing God's voice you cut everybody off and blamed the world when we didn't do things your way."

"Wayne, I – "

"Did you see the spelling of Am'rak's name in the newspaper? When they talked about his death?"

She sniffled, looked up at him and wiped her nose. "Huh?"

"Did you see how his name was spelled?"

"No?"

"Am'rak." He paused. "It spells karma backwards." He walked back to his garden and eased down to tend to his roses again. "Go home, Parade."

She stood up, dusted her knees and took a deep breath. "Wayne, I don't think I can do life without my best friend. Do you, do you think you could ever forgive me?"

SILENCE.

His back remained faced in her direction.

She looked down, took a deep breath and moved toward the gate.

"Time." He said.

She turned around and when she saw him tending to the ground she wondered if she was hearing things. "Did you say anything?"

"Give me time." He looked at her. "It's all I can offer for now."

Parade walked through the doors of her mansion where Jay was hanging up a portrait on the living room wall. "Where were you?" He asked. "You gotta start answering your phone because I'm still nervous about if anybody gonna come looking for what we did to Am'rak and his aunt. I mean, Mercer still got the blame for killing Danny and his family but I still don't feel safe."

"Where the kids?"

"Over friends' houses." He moved closer. "I thought you and I could spend some alone time."

She walked inside. "Do you truly love me, Jay?"

He smirked. "I already forgave you for fucking ole' boy so let it go."

"I asked you a question from the heart," she said seriously. "Do you love me? Or are you still manipulating the little girl whose only world revolved around you at Quincy Manor?"

"Parade, you asking me that question after I almost died for you? After everything we lost?"

"Jay, I'm tired. I'm tired of chasing images of women I think you want instead of me. I'm gonna lose my shape with age. I'm gonna lose my looks with time and I want to know when I do if you'll still be here."

Jay took a deep breath and moved closer. The last thing he wanted was his wife to feel inadequate. But Parade was out of pocket in his firm opinion. He got with her in the beginning because she was submissive and followed his lead but now...well now she was different.

"I almost died because you out here tossing pussy around and you come at me crazy?" He paused. "Are you serious?"

"You haven't answered my — "

"I don't owe you no fucking explanations!" He yelled. "You my wife and you will follow me blindly!"

Parade stumbled backwards. Jay had revealed his younger self just like she had revealed her immaturity earlier with Wayne. It was obvious that neither had grown much.

"I'll be back for my things in the morning," she said. "We can figure out what to do with the kids. I'm gonna stay at my shop for the time being but know that I want a divorce." She turned to walk out.

She realized in the moment that she needed time to figure out who she was outside of Jay. Good thing they took five hundred stacks out of Am'rak's house because she was able to rebuild her business and afford a place to stay.

More than all, in that moment, she realized Wayne was right. She wasn't sure who she was and what she wanted in the world. She did know that she didn't want to chase being someone else anymore. It was time to learn the real Parade. And although she wanted to take the journey with Jay he was too selfish in the moment and absorbed to take the journey with her.

She was almost to her car when he said, "Parade!"

She turned around where Jay was standing at the doorway. She swallowed the lump in her throat. "Yes."

"Don't leave me."

"I...this isn't...I can't..."

"Please." He moved closer. "You so wrong, Parade. So wrong about so many things."

"I'm confused."

He walked up to her. "I knew I loved you the moment..." He took a deep breath and squeezed her hand. "There has never been a woman I wanted, dead or alive, more than I wanted you. Ever." He paused. "Even cut my own mother off after hearing how she treated you and lied about me paying rent before the accident. I don't play when it comes to you. You it for me. And vice versa."

"But sometimes it feels...I mean..."

"If you feel like that's not the case then, baby, that's on me." He paused. "But I know this," he pointed at the ground, "If you stay you will feel me. I will show you how much I love and want you. Just, please, please don't go. No more running. I'm tired and we're too old for the games."

She looked into his eyes trying to determine if he was honest but the last thing she wanted was to play the victim.

She was just as guilty as he was with a lot of things. "I don't know, Jay."

"Two months."

"Huh?"

"Two months is all I need to fight for love. If it doesn't work you can leave and I won't stop you. Can you give me that?"

CARTEL PUBLICATIONS
PRESENTS

The Cartel Publications Order Form

www.thecartelpublications.com

Inmates **ONLY** receive novels for $10.00 per book **PLUS** shipping fee **PER BOOK.**

(Mail Order **MUST** come from inmate directly to receive discount)

Shyt List 1	_____	$15.00
Shyt List 2	_____	$15.00
Shyt List 3	_____	$15.00
Shyt List 4	_____	$15.00
Shyt List 5	_____	$15.00
Pitbulls In A Skirt	_____	$15.00
Pitbulls In A Skirt 2	_____	$15.00
Pitbulls In A Skirt 3	_____	$15.00
Pitbulls In A Skirt 4	_____	$15.00
Pitbulls In A Skirt 5	_____	$15.00
Victoria's Secret	_____	$15.00
Poison 1	_____	$15.00
Poison 2	_____	$15.00
Hell Razor Honeys	_____	$15.00
Hell Razor Honeys 2	_____	$15.00
A Hustler's Son	_____	$15.00
A Hustler's Son 2	_____	$15.00
Black and Ugly	_____	$15.00
Black and Ugly As Ever	_____	$15.00
Ms Wayne & The Queens of DC **(LGBT)**	_____	$15.00
Black And The Ugliest	_____	$15.00
Year Of The Crackmom	_____	$15.00
Deadheads	_____	$15.00
The Face That Launched A	_____	$15.00
Thousand Bullets		
The Unusual Suspects	_____	$15.00
Paid In Blood	_____	$15.00
Raunchy	_____	$15.00
Raunchy 2	_____	$15.00
Raunchy 3	_____	$15.00
Mad Maxxx (4th Book Raunchy Series)	_____	$15.00
Quita's Dayscare Center	_____	$15.00
Quita's Dayscare Center 2	_____	$15.00
Pretty Kings	_____	$15.00
Pretty Kings 2	_____	$15.00
Pretty Kings 3	_____	$15.00
Pretty Kings 4	_____	$15.00
Silence Of The Nine	_____	$15.00
Silence Of The Nine 2	_____	$15.00
Silence Of The Nine 3	_____	$15.00
Prison Throne	_____	$15.00
Drunk & Hot Girls	_____	$15.00
Hersband Material **(LGBT)**	_____	$15.00
The End: How To Write A	_____	$15.00
Bestselling Novel In 30 Days (Non-Fiction Guide)		
Upscale Kittens	_____	$15.00
Wake & Bake Boys	_____	$15.00
Young & Dumb	_____	$15.00

T. STYLES

Young & Dumb 2: Vyce's Getback _____	$15.00
Tranny 911 **(LGBT)** _____	$15.00
Tranny 911: Dixie's Rise **(LGBT)** _____	$15.00
First Comes Love, Then Comes Murder _____	$15.00
Luxury Tax _____	$15.00
The Lying King _____	$15.00
Crazy Kind Of Love _____	$15.00
Goon _____	$15.00
And They Call Me God _____	$15.00
The Ungrateful Bastards _____	$15.00
Lipstick Dom **(LGBT)** _____	$15.00
A School of Dolls **(LGBT)** _____	$15.00
Hoetic Justice _____	$15.00
KALI: Raunchy Relived _____	$15.00
(5th Book in Raunchy Series)	
Skeezers _____	$15.00
Skeezers 2 _____	$15.00
You Kissed Me, Now I Own You _____	$15.00
Nefarious _____	$15.00
Redbone 3: The Rise of The Fold _____	$15.00
The Fold (4th Redbone Book) _____	$15.00
Clown Niggas _____	$15.00
The One You Shouldn't Trust _____	$15.00
The WHORE The Wind	
Blew My Way _____	$15.00
She Brings The Worst Kind _____	$15.00
The House That Crack Built _____	$15.00
The House That Crack Built 2 _____	$15.00
The House That Crack Built 3 _____	$15.00
Level Up **(LGBT)** _____	$15.00
Villains: It's Savage Season _____	$15.00
Gay For My Bae _____	$15.00

(**Redbone 1 & 2** are **NOT** Cartel Publications novels and if **ordered** the cost is **FULL** price of $15.00 **each. No Exceptions**.)

Please add $5.00 **PER BOOK** for shipping and handling. **Inmates** too!

The Cartel Publications * P.O. BOX 486 OWINGS MILLS MD 21117

Name: _____

Address: _____

City/State: _____

Contact/Email: _____

Please allow 7-10 BUSINESS days before shipping.
The Cartel Publications is NOT responsible for Prison Orders rejected!

NO RETURNS and NO REFUNDS.
NO PERSONAL CHECKS ACCEPTED
STAMPS NO LONGER ACCEPTED

BLACK AND THE *UGLIEST*